DEATH IN ALBERT PARK

By the Same Author:

'Carolus Deene' Novels:

COLD BLOOD
AT DEATH'S DOOR
DEATH OF COLD
DEAD FOR A DUCAT
DEAD MAN'S SHOES
A LOUSE FOR THE HANGMAN
OUR JUBILEE IS DEATH
JACK ON THE GALLOWS TREE
FURIOUS OLD WOMEN
A BONE AND A HANK OF HAIR
DIE ALL, DIE MERRILY
NOTHING LIKE BLOOD
CRACK OF DOOM

DEATH IN ALBERT PARK

Leo Bruce

Charles Scribner's Sons
New York

First American edition published by Charles Scribner's Sons, 1979

Library of Congress Cataloging in Publication Data

Croft-Cooke, Rupert 1903-
Death in Albert Park.
I. Title.
PZ3.C8742Ddf 1979 [PR6005.R673] 823'.9'12
ISBN 0-684-16267-9 79-12006

1 3 5 7 9 11 13 15 17 19 F/C 20 18 16 14 12 10 8 6 4 2

Printed in the United States of America

DEATH IN ALBERT PARK

One

THE first was Hester Starkey.

She knew as soon as she began descending Crabtree Avenue that someone was following her. She did not at first feel any threat in this, though she did not want to look round in case it might be Grace Buller.

Hester was forty-nine years old, a small neat person who was reputed to be something of a martinet at St. Olave's Ladies' College. Senior English mistress, and second in seniority only to Miss Cratchley, the head, she was one of those resolute women who seem to have no difficulty in making up their minds and sticking to their decisions. She would have been pretty but for her thin lips and pallor—the grey eyes were cool and attractive.

She had been kept late that evening by a series of small accidents and just as she was preparing to leave at a quarter past seven, Grace Buller, the games mistress, had started one of her interminable wordy quarrels. Hester had listened impatiently and without ceding a point had eventually left Grace sulky but silenced. Hester passed through the school gates at a few minutes to eight o'clock.

She hated this suburb of Albert Park. "Pretentious!" she had said a score of times looking at the solid Victorian houses. It lay in the remote South East of London, surrounded by Forest Hill, Crystal Palace, Dulwich and Lewisham, a place of grey bricks and houses with gloomy basements built for the prosperous middle classes of the 1880's. Though threatened by the approach of vast blocks of flats it had so far kept its hideous character because no district railway served its commuters. The park from which it took its name was a green patch of twelve acres where trees dripped on the asphalt paths and a few torn shrubs, intended to flower, had a dank and cheerless existence. This park had been opened by the Prince Consort—one of his last public acts—when the area was still almost rural, but had been quickly surrounded by streets of grey houses.

The park was locked at night, to Hester Starkey's annoyance for this meant an extra quarter of a mile on her way home. She lived with her brother at Blackheath and went by bus from the corner of Inverness Road, a long street of semi-detached houses running from the foot of Crabtree Avenue towards Lewisham. St. Olave's was a day-school and several of the staff had cars but Hester, who had never learned to drive, disliked the thought of being instructed and coming to school with an L plate on her car. She was not an L plate person, she once admitted, and the remark was remembered in the Common Room.

That evening, Thursday, February 8, was dark and chilly but there was no fog or snow or driving rain, such as she had known too often on her walks to the bus. The street lamps were infrequent in Crabtree

Avenue and she always hurried down its long decline, not because she was afraid but because she found it depressing. People, once home in an area like this, seemed not to like coming out again and the streets were deserted.

The school was darkened when she left it. A man and wife lived there as caretakers at night but no one else remained on the premises. Grace Buller had probably gone down to the gym for her bag (which, someone observed, looked more like a postman's sack than a handbag) and would come out on her motor-scooter in a moment. Unless it would not start again, in which case Grace would overtake Hester with those great strides of hers and clump along beside her to the bus.

No. The footsteps following Hester were not Grace's. They were light speedy footsteps—a man's. Hester braced herself to turn and see who had followed her for two hundred yards now, neither falling behind nor passing her, but keeping a steady two yards or so behind. At the next lamp-post she *would* turn and face this unpleasant pursuer once and for all.

But at the next lamp-post she did not turn. The end of the street was in sight and she decided to hurry on. After all, whoever it was had not molested her yet, why should he do so now? She would get to the corner of Inverness Road where people were passing and face him there. Give him a piece of her mind, too. It could not be a coincidence. The distance was too carefully kept for that. If he meant to snatch her bag he would find she had a firm grip on it and anyway she had only about three pounds with her. If he had any . . . other intentions she could look after herself. She greatly disliked the idea of screaming, causing a commotion, being in a street scene, but she would certainly scream if he attempted anything. There were lights on in nearly all the houses of Crabtree Avenue and it would only be a few moments before people came.

But in one house, which she was now approaching, there were no lights for it was empty. She had noticed it before and wondered vaguely how a house could stand empty, even in this district. Perhaps someone had recently died there.

It was in the front garden of this house that Hester Starkey's body was found next morning. She had been killed by a single downward stroke of some sharp weapon, a butcher's knife, probably, which had entered at the left shoulder and penetrated straight to the heart. It was a powerful but deft blow made by someone who had probably studied the matter. It had certainly been struck from behind and death had been almost instantaneous.

It was a particularly shocking murder and the Press gave it prominence. As far as could be seen there was no reasonable motive. When the body was found it had been in no way interfered with and Hester's bag still contained her purse, her keys, her cheque book, while on her wrist was a rather valuable watch. The murderer had simply stabbed her, dragged or carried her into the garden of the empty house, laid her under the hedge there and left her.

She was not a popular woman, at school or at home, but murders are not committed from mere dislike. No one could seriously suppose that poor Grace Buller, for instance, who was known to have rather emotional rows with Hester, would follow her from the school and stab her with a butcher's knife out of sheer exasperation.

The only person at all close to her was her brother, Eamon Starkey, but not the slightest suspicion could attach to him, for quite apart from the lack of any possible motive he, an actor, had been on the stage of a small experimental theatre in North-West London that evening and had stayed the night at the flat of a friend in Hampstead as he often did when he was working.

Detective Superintendent Stephen Dyke was rather surprisingly put in charge of the case, a man usually working on even more publicized crimes. It was felt to be a sign that this inexplicable murder of a schoolmistress in a suburb might have greater significance than at first appeared. Dyke was a big man, physically and in his profession, ruthless but efficient. His round, seemingly boneless face with the quick hard eyes staring out from above puffy cheeks was familiar to readers of several newspapers for he was reputed to have brought about more hangings than any other CID man.

He looked for a lead to come in one of two possible ways. Or perhaps, as so often happened, out of the blue. The first of those ways was from enquiries on the spot, from some circumstance connected with the physical act of murder or some clue to be picked up in the area. The second was from Hester Starkey's life, or someone connected with it.

He was a thorough man and left nothing to chance. The most minute examination was made of the scene of the murder. It was assumed that Hester had been stabbed as she walked down the pavement. The murderer probably knew the district well and had chosen this spot in front of an empty house, afterwards using its garden for a temporary place of concealment for the body. He did not seem to have acted precipitately, laying the body in a position where it was invisible from the road or from the windows of the houses adjoining the empty one (number 46).

Householders in neighbouring houses, and later throughout the whole of Crabtree Avenue, were questioned but with little result. One woman, a Mrs. Sparkett, living several doors away at number 42, thought she had 'heard something' adding that 'you could not call it a scream, really, but definitely something'. Further cross-examination proved that this 'something' had happened while Hester was still arguing with Grace Buller at the school.

Another would-be helpful resident, a man named Tuckman, had walked up the avenue an hour before the supposed time of the crime and had 'seen someone suspicious hanging about'. Pressed for details he admitted that the only cause for suspicion was that he had never seen the man before, and that the stranger was only 'hanging about' in the sense that he was looking for a house number. He turned out to be a chartered accountant searching for the home of a Mr. Goggins who lived at number 18.

The crew of every bus which stopped at the corner of Inverness Road at the relevant times were examined but these Jamaicans could supply little information, one saying frankly that all white people looked alike to him and another having an elaborate theory of the crime that he wanted to voice, but no details in the least helpful of the evening in question.

That the murderer had come in a car and left it somewhere in the district was a possibility which Dyke did not ignore but no car park attendant had noticed anything unusual. One had thought a man who drove off at about eight was the worse for drink, as he put it, but as Dyke was not at the moment concerned with a drunk-in-charge case this was not helpful. The murderer, with his cool aim and single downward stroke had been anything but drunk. No car, not customarily standing there at night, had been noticed in Crabtree Avenue or its immediate environs, though round in Perth Avenue there had been a party which had brought a couple of car loads.

The wife of the caretaker of St. Olave's had come up to the school at about 6:30 and at first raised everyone's hopes by saying it was funny, that was the night she thought she saw someone under the trees at the top of the avenue. She could have *sworn* there was someone hanging about there as she came to the school gates. What kind of person? Well, that she couldn't say. She hadn't stopped to look. Further questioned she admitted that it could have been one of the girls waiting there, or a policeman on duty, or just a trick of light and shadow, or nothing at all.

The park-keeper was no more helpful. He had made his last rounds at 6 o'clock as usual before locking up at 7. The park was kept open later in summer, he said, but what was the good of keeping open in this weather? It only led to mischief and even now some of the young couples found a way of getting over the railings at night as he had good reason to know from what he saw next morning. Yes, he had made his rounds and found no one in the park but an old gent who often came there in the evening and was, if you asked the park-keeper, a bit weak in the head but as harmless as a baby. Name? He seemed to think he'd heard him called Mr. Smithers, and somebody had once told him, though he couldn't be sure, that he lived in Cromarty Avenue.

Duly traced Mr. Smithers turned out to be the retired secretary of a charitable institution who had spent the evening playing bezique with his daughter-in-law. The park-keeper himself, an ex-soldier named

Slatter, lived in a lodge at the main gates of the park, which were on the side farthest from Crabtree Avenue, and had heard nothing.

Bloodstains were found at the scene of the murder but examination proved them to be of Hester's blood group. The weapon was missing but examination of the body confirmed that it was a sharp and powerful knife or dagger, wielded from behind the victim. Routine enquiries were ordered in connection with this but yielded nothing. There was also the possibility that bloodstains were on the murderer's clothes and this led to the usual alert to cleaning firms, but again with no result.

Everyone was, as usual, too anxious to be helpful, too full of details of no possible relevance. A couple of lunatics came forward, according to precedent, to confess that they had committed the crime, but one of these had been in Bristol at the time and the other had confessed to every major murder since the Green Bicycle Case. Local enquiries in fact failed to produce anything to go on and after an Inquest had found it was a case of murder against a person or persons unknown, Hester was buried in the local cemetery, the senior girls from St. Olave's, with express permission from their parents, attending the ceremony and weeping as they had never thought to do at the departure of "The Stark".

Dyke's more personal enquiries led to little enlightenment. He found Hester's brother Eamon a particularly irritating man, not too intelligent but with an excellent opinion of himself. He had already given statements to every newspaper which would agree to publish his picture and to mention the name of the play in which he was appearing. His sister, he told Dyke, was a woman of dominant personality but so far as he knew she had no enemies. Her only friend was a fellow-teacher at St. Olave's, a Miss Gerda Munshall, with whom Hester took her summer holidays abroad. There were no near relatives beyond the usual aunt in St. Leonards-on-Sea and a cousin of the father's, a rich woman called Dobson, from whom there were vague expectations. Eamon Starkey thought, as he airily smoked a cigarette, that his sister had probably been murdered by a sex-maniac and wondered that the police left such people at large.

Poor Grace Buller, a very large young woman with spaniel eyes and mighty calves, found it difficult to answer questions because she wept too easily and remembered that the last words she exchanged with Hester were bitter ones. She gave a full account of the quarrel and lamented that but for her motor-scooter failing to start she might have been on the spot to save Hester. She had, in fact, ridden home twenty minutes after parting from Hester and 'must have passed the very spot soon after it happened'. More tears. Hester, she added gratuitously, was the last person you would expect to be murdered. Why? Well, she was. You'd never have believed it possible. She was so . . . self-possessed.

Dyke's toughest interview was with Miss Cratchley, the headmistress, a remarkable woman who had ruled the school for eighteen years and was not going to lose her poise over the murder of her senior assistant or the intrusion of a senior policeman. She gave Dyke an interview as soon as he asked for it but made it plain that it was to be on her own terms and in her own study. Long able to intimidate staff and parents alike, not to mention her pupils, she anticipated no trouble from a Detective Superintendent and began by telling Dyke that he was wasting his time in making enquiries at the school.

"What in the world do you expect to find here?" she asked haughtily. "A plot by my senior girls to get rid of an unpopular mistress?"

"That's not quite the point, Miss Cratchley."

"Then what is the point? The girls see you round the place and have quite enough *nous* to know what you are. It's liable to start the wildest stories. Already I have had parents ringing up to ask if their children are going to be questioned."

"They may have to be," threatened Dyke.

"Rubbish," said Miss Cratchley, getting a deal of expression into her pronunciation of the word. "What on earth could the girls know about it? They were all at home long before Hester left the school that evening."

"In a case like this . . ."

"May I ask if you've ever *had* a case like this, Superintendent?"

"Not exactly the same, of course, but we've had women being stabbed before in very similar circumstances."

"Oh, you have. With no possible motive of gain? With no evidence of any sexual aberration on the part of the murderer? With no passion or jealousy or hatred involved?"

"As for those three, we have no evidence in this case either way. But they can supply a motive in the most extraordinary cases. A woman does not need to be young and attractive to rouse passion, or jealousy or hatred, as you name them."

"I see. So you think poor Hester Starkey was a *femme fatale*, Superintendent?"

"I said there was no evidence either way."

"But you infer that she may have been. You did not know her, you see. She was cold and utterly self-sufficient. A clever teacher, oh yes. A woman of some organizing ability, when properly directed. But no more capable of arousing passion of any kind than a brick wall. No, my dear Superintendent. You are barking up the wrong tree. Look outside for your murderer and remember that it was chance which made him pick on Hester. Pure chance. He is a man with a lust for killing, that's all. A Jack the Ripper. It is the only possible explanation."

Dyke, who was already secretly inclined to agree with her, nodded and went on to routine questions.

But the name was out in his mind. Jack the Ripper. Or the Stabber, in this case. Someone, man or woman, with a lunatic urge to slay. Someone who left no trace because he had no motive connected with a particular victim.

If this were the case, the very ugly case, it was fairly certain that somewhere, not too far away or too long a time hence, he would strike again.

Two

THE second was Joyce Ribbing.

Her body was seen from the front window of number 18 Crabtree Avenue by Lionel Goggins the tenant. He was a big ponderous man and his deep voice was known to his neighbours for he had a way of shouting at anyone he met on his way to the station in the morning.

On the morning of February 23 he drew back the curtains across the bay window of his front bedroom and said to his wife—"There's something in the garden."

The night had been misty and had turned to fine rain in the small hours but now, at 8:30, the visibility was good.

"What is it?" asked his wife, yawning.

"Well, it looks to me like a corpse," boomed Mr. Goggins. "A woman's corpse."

"Not another murder!" pleaded Ada Goggins.

"That's what it looks like. Unless the woman's been taken ill. I'll go down and investigate."

"Wrap up well, dear. You don't want one of your chills."

Lionel Goggins obeyed but it did not take him many moments to discover the truth.

"It's Joyce Ribbing," he told his wife.

"Well don't leave her out there. It's raining."

"She's dead," said Lionel Goggins, and went straight to the bathroom to be sick.

His wife waited impatiently. Lionel was prone to fits of nausea.

"What do you mean 'dead'?" asked Ada sharply on his return. "She can't be dead. I was playing Bridge with her last night."

"She's dead," repeated Lionel. "I must phone the police. She has been stabbed, I think. In the left shoulder."

"Then it *is* another murder!" discovered Ada. "That's how that schoolmistress was killed a few doors away. It means there's a killer at work in this street. You'd better do something, Lionel. You can't leave her lying out there in the rain, even if she is dead."

"She mustn't be touched," said Goggins, "till the police have been. They'll see to all that."

"Phone them, then. And phone her husband. He must be wondering where she is."

To say that John Ribbing, the local doctor, was 'wondering' was to put it mildly. When his wife had failed to return at eleven o'clock on the previous evening he phoned Mrs. Whitehill in whose house she was playing Bridge and learned that she had left there two hours earlier with the intention as she had said of 'running' home. The Ribbings lived in Perth Avenue, not three hundred yards away, and Joyce was an active woman in her early forties who should have covered the distance in less than five minutes. Yet John Ribbing hesitated to call the police because of Raymond Turrell. This was a somewhat younger man with whom Joyce had been friendly lately. What John Ribbing feared, and almost believed, was that Turrell had been waiting in his car outside the Whitehills' house and had taken Joyce to his flat in Chelsea.

His indecision was ended by a call from Mrs. Whitehill.

"Joyce back yet?" she asked briskly.

"No."

"I thought I'd just ask. We feel rather anxious about it. She said she was going straight home."

"Yes. I'm worried."

"You see . . . I don't want to put ideas in your head, doctor, but there was that dreadful business of the schoolmistress a few weeks ago."

"Good God! You don't think . . ."

"I don't think anything. But you should call the police, perhaps."

He did so with the result that a squad car was soon outside his house and he was explaining to a sympathetic young detective sergeant. He felt he could not leave Raymond Turrell out of it.

"We'll soon settle that part of it," said the young man. "Someone will call on Turrell straight away. Now is there nothing else you can suggest?"

"Unless she has gone down to her sister at Sevenoaks."

"Any reason why she should?"

"None. She said she was coming straight home. She would have had to get a car for the journey. We have only the one and that's in the garage."

"We can cross that off then. At any rate for the time being. Anything else?"

"There was this murder," said John Ribbing miserably.

"I don't think we need worry about that, for the moment, anyway. Lightning does not strike in the same place twice."

"But if . . ."

"We must find your wife, doctor, not suppose anything of that sort. Now, her description please . . ."

It had been a ghastly night for Ribbing. The report concerning Turrell was, when it came through, negative, as the young detective said. He had satisfactorily accounted for his movements that evening. There was nothing to do but wait and thank heaven that the children were away at school.

It was not until nearly 9 o'clock in the morning that Lionel Goggins told him the truth.

"I'll come round at once," he said in the words he had so often used to the anxious relatives of patients.

But the police were before him. He was in time to recognize the body of Joyce where it still lay pathetically in the rain, not much protected by a privet hedge; then he was led indoors by Lionel Goggins and given brandy.

The investigation this time was on simpler lines for Dyke did not waste much attention on Joyce and her background, but concentrated on details which might help to find the killer. Some enquiries were made by one of Dyke's assistants, however, and these brought to light a rather sordid state of affairs. Raymond Turrell at first denied that his friendship with Joyce was more than casual. He had met her one morning last autumn when they had both been shopping at a famous department store in Kensington and had seen one another from time to time since. Pressed further he admitted that

Joyce had been to his flat and finally that they were lovers. But he denied that they had any plans for the future. Joyce had her obligations to her husband and children and so far as he knew had never thought of leaving them. Asked if Dr. Ribbing knew of the affair, he hedged somewhat, then said 'Probably'. What did he mean by that? He meant that Joyce had told him she believed her husband had found out, though he had not said anything yet. He had last seen Joyce a week ago and they had not discussed the murder of Hester Starkey.

"I've never been much interested in murder cases," said Turrell. "Anyway, that seemed a very ordinary one. Women are always getting stabbed or strangled. It was nothing to do with us."

"And now?"

"It's different, of course," said Turrell sadly.

Joyce's sister in Sevenoaks was also interviewed. She had known of Joyce's affair with Turrell but had not taken it very seriously. It would have blown over. Joyce was very fond of her husband and children.

Bridge at Mrs. Whitehill's that evening had lasted from 4:30 till 8 o'clock. The players were all women, Mrs. Whitehill, Joyce Ribbing, Ada Goggins and Mrs. Whitehill's niece Viola. The time of Joyce's leaving the house was not noted exactly but it was fixed at between 8:45 and 9 o'clock because Mrs. Whitehill remembered the clock in the hall striking just after Joyce said she really must fly. Joyce had left 'quite cheerful, quite herself,' making some little joking remark about neglecting her husband and had hurried away. Mrs. Goggins? She had stayed almost another hour, 'having something to eat' with Mrs. Whitehill. She lived only a few doors away.

Among the residents in Crabtree Avenue, if not among the investigating police, a question began to be asked. Why had nothing been heard of either murder at the time? In the second particularly, when Joyce knew what had happened in this avenue three weeks earlier, surely she must have screamed when she became aware of someone following her? Could it be that this someone was known to her, that she had perhaps waited for him to catch her up, that the Stabber (as he had come to be called) was actually a resident in the avenue or someone known to most of them?

Dyke thought it wise to dispel this to some extent by giving a piece of information to John Ribbing. Examination of the body and certain minutiae round the mouth and neck suggested that Joyce had been gagged before she was stabbed. Perhaps someone had approached her and before she could call for help had muffled her with a woollen scarf (a grey woollen scarf, it appeared from microscopic examination) which he held ready, and had then stabbed her.

Though it was admitted, when this was known, that the Stabber might be someone previously unseen by his victims, the idea that it might be a local resident was not completely abandoned and some ugly suspicions began to grow. There were householders in Crabtree Avenue who 'kept themselves to themselves' and even on the way to the station in the morning did not join in general greetings and discussion of last night's television programmes. There were people about whom nothing was known, and people of whom it could be said 'I've always thought there was *something*,' and people who were rather disliked for their aloofness or failure to conform to the social standards of the avenue. So instead of these prejudices being forgotten in the common emergency, the fact that the Stabber might be a local gave them point.

A great deal of sympathy went to Dr. Ribbing, who had always been a popular man, and there were bitter remarks about the police when it was known that he had been questioned twice.

"A pity they don't get this madman with the knife instead of pestering the poor doctor with questions," was said more than once.

Ribbing had, of course, been able to account for all his movements that evening but even Detective Superintendent Dyke seemed to think this was a formality. He questioned other residents with as much pertinacity as before, and with as little result. No one had seen a stranger in the avenue that evening, no one had heard an unusual sound, and no strange car was reported to have been waiting in the neighbourhood. The weapon had not been found though medical examination decided that 'almost certainly' it was the weapon used for the murder of Hester Starkey.

So now a picture was beginning to form in the minds of the more imaginative residents and it was a very horrible one. Someone, almost certainly a man, waited on dark or misty nights among the trees of Crabtree Avenue, or perhaps in one of the more shadowed gardens, or among the trees by the school gates at the top of the avenue. He was armed with a butcher's knife, a powerful blade at least ten inches in length. He was either a raving madman, or, more probably and more fearfully, a schizophrenic, a Jekyll-and-Hyde, who could appear perfectly normal at other times. He was waiting for a woman to appear alone at a time when the street was deserted. Any woman, it was thought, for the only thing that Hester Starkey and Joyce Ribbing had in common was that both were a little less than average in height. His mania was to strike, to kill, and no more.

A Mr. Tuckman, a city man at number 24, was reputed to be something of a psychologist and was listened to on this.

"Although the urge is certainly pathological, and must have some sexual basis, this is no ordinary sex-maniac. The bodies were not mutilated in any way."

But this gave no reassurance to the residents who were growing increasingly apprehensive. The police were much abused though no one could suggest what might have been done to prevent the second murder, unless it was to make an arrest after the first.

"If they had done that," boomed Goggins a little obviously, "Joyce Ribbing would be alive today."

Precautions were, of course, taken by Dyke, though the nature of these were not revealed. A special patrol of the uniformed police covered the avenue from lighting-up time till the small hours of the morning, and there were other steps secretly taken to safeguard those who had to use the avenue at night. But the residents themselves were their own chief protection.

On the night after Joyce Ribbing's funeral, Alec Tuckman called together what he called a nucleus of those concerned and suggested that the men should form themselves into a body of Vigilantes. These would be available "to escort women, to keep their eyes and ears open, and to try to buck up the police a bit," so that the district could be itself again. He, Whitehill, (an occulist and rather an obscure character sent by his wife to Tuckman's meeting,) Goggins, a man named Heatherwell from number 32, and a young insurance agent named Gates who lived with his aged parents at number 52, agreed to this and it was hoped to increase the force.

The Crabtree Vigilantes received their rebuffs, however. The Press, though not openly ridiculing them, gave them such prominence that they could not carry out their simple programme unmolested, and the fact that local residents had been forced to form a Vigilante society was made to reflect on the police. When Turnwright, a somewhat vulgar character from number 28, was asked to join, he retorted with ill-timed flippancy, his reply being considered in the worst possible taste.

"Vigilantes?" he said to Goggins. "What the hell for? For twenty years I've been trying to get rid of my old woman—d'you think I'm going to spoil my chances now?"

But in spite of such set-backs the Vigilantes set to work and there was a good deal of telephoning between their houses and even a search, by three of them with torches, of front gardens in the avenue on a particularly murky night.

All this did not relieve the very real horror of the situation. There really was some kind of madman about and he had evidently chosen this quiet avenue for his assassinations. There really was danger, particularly it would seem for women, but also, it might be, for men. A certain apprehension surrounded the Park. One side of Crabtree Avenue was open to it and though the railings were close together, pointed and tall, it was felt that they would not be sufficient to exclude the kind of demon the Stabber might be. A certain confusion perhaps existed between those two lethal Jacks of the last century, Spring-Heel Jack and Jack the Ripper. The Stabber was rapidly becoming a legend.

"The only way I can see in which he may be caught," said Tuckman importantly, "is *in flagrante delicto*. Jack the Ripper was never caught. A man who seeks only to *kill*, without any ulterior motive, is almost undiscoverable unless he can be taken in the act. None of the ordinary rules of detection apply."

"In that case you think some other poor woman . . ."

"Not necessarily. We may be lucky enough to catch him before he does it."

There was an unfortunate sequel to this. A few nights later when Tuckman, Whitehill and young Gates were making what Tuckman called a routine patrol of the avenue, they saw a 'mysterious figure' ahead of them, a man in a felt hat and a raincoat which was buttoned high against the wet and driving wind. His movements from the first were highly questionable, he "seemed to materialize" from the trees near the school gates and start down the pavement in an abstracted way. When he approached the empty house the three Vigilantes stopped to watch him and when he actually pushed open the gate and disappeared into the garden they became tense and perhaps somewhat over-excited.

"We've got him," whispered Tuckman. "He can't get out of there unless he has a key of the house or the side-door. Come on!"

They went and found the stranger standing on the overgrown small lawn of the empty house gazing about him. With a rush the three were upon him and in the scuffle the stranger went to the ground.

"Call the police!" shouted Tuckman.

"I *am* the police," said the stranger mildly, from underneath young Gates.

And so it was. There were apologies and regrets for a 'little misunderstanding' but the incident did nothing to improve the already strained relations between the residents and the Law. Dyke became a somewhat rude and savage man. This was, he said, the *hell* of a case. There was nothing to get hold of and every prospect of another lethal attack on a woman. Not all the patrolling he could give to the district could eliminate the possibility of this and another corpse would blast his own reputation and that of the police. Yet what more could he do to prevent it? His only chance was to find some clue to the Stabber's identity and so far none, absolutely none, had come to light.

Three

THE third was . . . but before there was a third victim, the case aroused the interest of Carolus Deene.

This was scarcely to be wondered at, for the Stabber was the most widely discussed murderer since Christie. That case had reached headlines only after the victims were found and the murderer arrested; this received its daily measure of newsprint while the murders were still, as it were, going on, and newspapers could scarcely refrain from speculating on who might be the next unfortunate woman to be stabbed.

Crabtree Avenue, a few weeks before one of hundreds of ugly Victorian streets in the suburbs, had become famous and pictures of it had appeared in most of the national newspapers. Number 46, the Empty House, in the garden of which Hester Starkey's body had been discovered, first appeared and it was a matter of some disappointment that Number 18, the home of Lionel and Ada Goggins was almost a replica of it. Lionel Goggins who had discovered the second body in his front garden had, however, looked solemnly out of news sheets.

That two weeks precisely separated the two murders was noticed and there was a school of thought which argued that the third would be attempted fourteen days after the death of Joyce. Others sought some connection with the moon. One newspaper published a picture of a butcher's knife with a caption asking the public to report the discovery of such a weapon or anything connected with it. Various names were attached to the murderer, the most popular being the simplest—the Stabber. Letters in the more serious newspapers began to appear, not signed as in the last century *Vox Populi* or *Pro Bono Publico* but bearing the names of several quite eminent people. Questions were asked in the House calculated to embarrass the Home Secretary—what steps was he taking to protect, and so on, and the Home Secretary stated that he did not think it wise to discuss his Security measures but would be glad to give the Leader of the Opposition the fullest details in a private interview.

The case, in fact, fell somewhere between a Scandal and a Sensation and its many side-issues received publicity. Mr. Turnwright explained why he would not join the Vigilantes ("Don't believe in that sort of thing myself") and Mrs. Whitehill once again described Joyce Ribbing's departure from the Bridge party.

But there is a limit to the possibilities of daily reporting on one theme and after ten days had passed there was a lull in the affairs of Crabtree Avenue until, on the morning of the fourteenth day, readers were faced with the question "Will He Strike Again?" together with details of some of the precautions taken to prevent any fresh outrage. On the fifteenth, when no new crime was reported, it was surmised that police vigilance, together with the combined action of householders, had prevented the Stabber from carrying out yet another murder.

It was at this point, when public interest seemed for the moment to have evaporated, that Carolus Deene began to interest himself in the case from a distance of sixty miles.

Perhaps some special concern came from the fact that he was, like Hester Starkey, a member of a school staff, being Senior History Master at the Queen's School, Newminster, a small but ancient institution in a Cathedral city.

He was by no means a conventional schoolmaster. His father had left him a rich man and although not greatly interested in wealth he had found, like so many of his kind, that it accumulated rather than grew less. Leaving his affairs to a firm of stockbrokers in which a boyhood friend was partner he had the responsibility of increasing riches forced on him. He was generous to others and allowed himself his fads, including a Bentley Continental and a small Queen Anne house with a charming walled garden near the cathedral.

His girl wife had been killed in an air raid and since his own release, Carolus had been looked after by a middle-aged couple named Stick, Mrs. Stick being that phenomenon among Englishwomen of her class, an inspired and imaginative cook. The years had passed pleasantly in Newminster for Carolus, who had returned to teaching after the war rather than face the boredom of idleness, enjoyed his work at the school and enjoyed his own well-ordered private life.

The Queen's School, Newminster, is, as its pupils find themselves under the necessity rather often of explaining, a public school. A minor, a small, a lesser-known one, they concede, but still in the required category. Its buildings are old, picturesque and very unhygienic, and one of its classrooms is a showpiece untouched from the Elizabethan age in which the school was founded.

Some years before this time the school had been given a little reflected fame, for Carolus Deene published a a successful book and did not scorn to print under his name 'Senior History Master at the Queen's School, Newminster'. The book was called *Who Killed William Rufus? And Other Mysteries of History*, and in it Deene most ingeniously applied the methods of a modern detective to some of the more spectacular crimes of the past and in more than one case seemed to have found new evidence from which to draw startling conclusions. On the Princes in the Tower he was particularly original and perceptive and he disposed of much unreliable detail in his study of the murder of Edward II. The book was highly praised and sold a number of editions.

"It doesn't, unfortunately, make Deene a good disciplinarian," said the headmaster. "His class is the noisiest rabble in the school."

Carolus Deene was forty years old. He had been a good all-round athlete with a half-blue for boxing and a fine record in athletics. During the war he did violent things, always with a certain elegance for which he was famous. He jumped out of aeroplanes with a parachute and actually killed a couple of men with his Commando knife which he supposed ingenuously, had been issued to him for that purpose."

He was slim, dapper, rather pale and he dressed too well for a schoolmaster. He was not a good disciplinarian as the headmaster understood the word, because he simply could not be bothered with discipline, being far too interested in his subject. If there were stupid boys who did not feel this interest and preferred to sit at the back of his class and eat revolting sweets and hold whispered conversations on county cricket, then he let them, continuing to talk to the few who listened. He was popular but considered a little odd. His dressiness and passionate interest in both history and crime were his best known characteristics in the school, though among the staff his large private income was a matter for some invidious comment.

The boys were apt to take advantage of his known interest in crime both ancient and modern. A master with a hobby-horse is easily led away from the tiresome lesson in hand into the realms of his fancy. He may or may not realize this as the end of the school period comes and he finds that he has talked for three-quarters of an hour on his favourite subject and forgotten what he was supposed to be teaching.

Carolus Deene was very well aware of his weakness but he regarded his twin interests of crime and history as almost indistinguishable. The history of men is the history of their crimes, he said. Crippen and Richard III, Nero and the latest murderer to be given headlines in newspapers were all one to him, as his pupils delightedly discovered.

Some years earlier he had become involved in the solving of a local murder mystery because the detective in charge had been a friend of his whom he wanted to help, and this had led him to other cases in which, in a self-effacing way, he had been of material help to the investigating police, who rarely appreciated what looked like interference. One or two had valued his theorizing but Carolus was actuated by a passion for puzzle-solving and wanted no recognition. He tackled murders as he tackled a stiff crossword puzzle and was rarely defeated by either.

The attitude of the headmaster, Mr. Hugh Gorringer, to his researches into modern crime was a mixed one. A large and somewhat pompous man, with a vast store of old-fashioned clichés on which to draw in conversation, he had at first thoroughly disapproved of one of his assistants becoming, as he called it, 'embroiled in such squalid matters.' He had large red ears, hairy as a pachyderm's, and to these, he claimed, it had come, when Carolus showed too lively an interest in an unsolved mystery. Then he would appeal to Carolus to remember the good name of the Queen's School and not allow any 'adverse publicity' to touch it. On the other hand Mr. Gorringer had a very human curiosity in such matters and had frequently "lent his presence" to the closing acts of a criminal drama on the plea of protecting the reputation of his school.

During that Spring term, when the newspaper-reading public was being given the two successive shocks of the murders in Crabtree Avenue, Carolus had become aware of a certain watchfulness in Mr. Gorringer as though he feared the worst. When the headmaster's apprehensive curiosity could be contained no longer, he fell into step with Carolus as the two crossed the quadrangle from chapel.

"Ah, Deene," said Mr. Gorringer, "I wanted a word with you. A bird has whispered in my ear . . ." Carolus wondered, and not for the first time, what huge carrion hawk or vulture could have perched on that shoulder and croaked into that hairy cavern . . . "that you have expressed some curiosity about certain events of a violent nature in the suburb of Albert Park."

"Yes. Beastly case, isn't it?"

"Tragic," said Mr. Gorringer. "Tragic. When lunacy and crime join hands . . ." he shook his head expressively. "Do you think there will be further . . . incidents?"

"How can one possibly tell?"

"There was, alas, a certain pattern in these two brutal killings which makes an unskilled observer like me fear the worst. Yet the strictest precautions must have been taken. You have no theory, Deene?"

"Theory? No. I've only read the newspaper accounts."

"I thought that with your *penchant* for such affairs you might have evolved some ingenious concept of your own. However, I am relieved to find you have so little interest in the matter."

"I didn't say I wasn't interested, headmaster. I said I had no theory."

Mr. Gorringer stopped dramatically.

"Deene! You are not proposing to involve yourself in such sordid and highly publicized occurrences?"

"I hadn't really thought about it. There's another week of term yet, and I should think it would all be cleared up during that time."

Mr. Gorringer cleared his throat.

"I fear I must make my position absolutely clear," he said. "I have heretofore—if not acquiesced, at least turned a blind eye when you, a senior assistant at my school, have endangered its fair name by your participation in matters best left to the police. In this case, with every newspaper crying aloud the unpleasant details, it would be disastrous, nothing short of disastrous, for you to become involved. I must, in fact, apply the veto which I feel empowered to use. I must ask you, as you value our amicable relationship, to abandon all thought of . . . investigation."

"But suppose I saw a way of preventing another murder? Will you take the responsibility then?"

"Assuredly I will. As tax-payers we employ skilled public servants . . ."

"I know. But you can't employ ideas. I'll agree to this much, headmaster. If there is not another of these murders between now and the end of term I will drop the thing. But if there is, and with it a prospect of yet another, I shall really feel it my duty at least to have a try. It's just possible that I might hit on something helpful."

"Ah, Deene, Deene, you place me in a truly embarrassing situation. You would have me feel that blood is on my hands. But I will accept your conditions. Should there be another murder, unquestionably a sequel to the first two, during these next three weeks, I absolve you from my ban, and you must add your mite to the quota of intelligence being applied to this case. But I fervently pray that we have heard the last of Crabtree Avenue. I think I see our excellent music master approaching. I must have a word with him. Ah, Tubley . . ."

It was four days later that the third victim fell, on March 15. Not this time in the closely guarded Crabtree Avenue but within half a mile of it, on the other side of Albert Park, in a similar street called Salisbury Gardens. A Mrs. Crabbett was found stabbed in precisely the same manner, by the same kind of weapon. Her body, like those of her predecessors, had been laid in the front garden of a house overshadowed by trees. Her death had taken place at approximately the same hour as Hester Starkey's, in the region of eight o'clock. She too had been muffled by a grey woollen scarf before she was stabbed.

This time public feeling became vociferous and a leader appeared in *The Times*. There were no more covert sneers about the Crabtree Vigilantes but a mass meeting of residents in the whole area to consider what should be done. People went about the suburb, and the neighbouring suburb, with anxious faces, and reminded one another that you could not tell who would be next. The husband of the dead woman received hundreds of letters of condolence, and although more thoughtful people did not blame the police, popular abuse of them was unrestrained. What were they doing? Why had they not made an arrest in the first two cases? Was no woman safe in the street at night? Did the police intend to wait till this maniac grew tired or died, as Jack the Ripper had done, remaining undiscovered to the end?

The circumstances in the case were straightforward. The Crabbetts, an elderly couple, lived in Bromley where they had a flat in a new building. Mr. Crabbett was vaguely known to be 'retired' and Mrs. Crabbett was considered by her friends to have in common with the other two murdered women that she was a self-possessed rather masterful woman, not likely to be easily scared. Her husband was doubly distressed for apart from his loss—they had been married for over thirty years—he blamed himself for not having brought his wife home that evening as arranged. She had been to visit her married daughter, Isobel Pressley, who lived in Salisbury Gardens, and Jim Crabbett her husband had arranged to call for her in their Ford Prefect car at seven. He was however, a notoriously vague and unreliable person and had reached his daughter's house at eight, to hear his wife had lost patience and gone home. She would walk down the road, she said, and catch a bus from the bottom which would take her to Bromley.

Alarm at the Stabber's activities had chiefly centred on Crabtree Avenue at this time and it had not occurred to her or her daughter that there might be danger so far away.

Jim Crabbett had returned to Bromley and when his wife had failed to appear at 10 o'clock had telephoned the police. Detective Superintendent Dyke had been informed, and a search had at once been ordered, both in Crabtree Avenue and Salisbury Gardens and at a little after midnight Mrs. Crabbett's body had been found.

There was, however, in this case an important witness. A Miss Pilkin, who lived in first floor apartments of the house opposite the Pressleys had some kind of a feud with them connected with her Pomeranian dog. Like many elderly women living alone, she enjoyed this and a part of her enjoyment came from a close observation of 'those opposite'. She knew to the moment what time Harry Pressley should arrive from the city and was prepared to believe that there was trouble behind drawn blinds across the road if he was late. If the Pressleys did not draw their curtains Miss Pilkin would creep into her dark front room and take up her position, not too near the window. As there was a streetlight fairly close to the Pressleys' home, she was able to observe comings and goings, and knew of the occasional visits of Mrs. Crabbett.

That evening, for instance, she had seen Mrs. Crabbett arrive in time for tea and had noted that Harry Pressley came home as usual at a little before 6. She had seen Mrs. Crabbett depart at about 7:45 and Mr. Crabbett, whom she also knew by sight, arrive soon after 8 and shortly leave again. But what interested Dyke most in her evidence was her story of a man in a cloth cap and a raincoat, wearing glasses and carrying a newspaper who was 'hanging about' in the street that evening. She had taken note of him because he looked rather odd. Odd? Yes, his raincoat was too large for him. Time? She would say it was about 7 when she had seen him first but he had come back several times. He seemed to be waiting for someone.

This was at last a lead and Dyke put out further enquiries for anyone who might have seen the stranger. He sent a man to call at every house in Salisbury Gardens to make enquiries about him, but received only the usual conflicting evidence. One woman believed she had seen the man several nights ago and had thought at the time there was something she did not like about him, while another resident was sure he had sat near him on a bus that day.

Pressed for further description Miss Pilkin thought the man was of 'medium height', and, she would think, middling in age. He hadn't given her the impression of being *young*, but then again she wouldn't say he was *old*. There was nothing much else she had noticed about him, except she was sure he had not called at the Pressleys'. She would have noticed that, she said. She had not liked the Pressleys, she admitted, but she was sorry now, because it was terrible about Mrs. Crabbett. She wouldn't want anything like that to happen to anyone. They had been unkind to her dog, and she couldn't forget it, because her dog would never hurt anyone and had only wanted to play with the Pressleys' little girl. Still, that was one thing and murder was another and she wouldn't like anyone to think she had wished it on her. As for that man she had seen, she herself was quite sure it was the Stabber, now she came to think of it. She meant, who else could it be hanging about there? But she had not thought of it at the time because the Stabber belonged on the other side of the Park and she wasn't one to think the worst of people. If she had, she'd have warned Mrs. Crabbett instead of letting her go straight to her death like that, poor thing. She *had* thought there was something unpleasant about the man she had seen. He had a bad aura, she said. But she had never connected him with the murders.

Once again there were bloodstains, but no weapon. Once again no motive could be found for anyone but a homicidal lunatic. Once again there was nothing in the dead woman's life that was not commonplace. Once again there was nothing to suggest any dark sexual aspect of the affair. Once again there seemed to be no way of identifying the madman or preventing him from striking again.

"Well, Deene," said Mr. Gorringer with assumed mournfulness. "I suppose you will now insist on your part of our bargain. You will want your pound of flesh, if that is not too unhappily apt a metaphor to use."

"I am certainly going to spend the holidays, or part of them, in Albert Park."

"I feared it. But my hands are tied. Tell me, though, have you any predisposition in the matter? Any inkling of how to go about it? It is indeed a baffling problem—a lunatic at large, a creature perhaps appearing normal in his everyday life. How will you start?"

"Oh, exactly as I always do. Make a few enquiries in each case. Try to get the background."

"But surely here, the background of the unfortunate victims is of secondary interest? It probably was not even known to the murderer."

"That may be. But I know no other way. I shall treat each case *as* a case of murder."

"You mean, you don't think they are all the work of one madman?"

"I don't say that. They well may be. But I don't think that should be assumed too readily. I propose to take them one by one. I have a feeling I shall come on something. Perhaps find something as yet unnoticed which is common to all."

"I trust you will preserve the strictest anonymity, Deene?"

"You needn't worry about that. The school won't be mentioned. In fact, I may as well tell you, headmaster, that I have never felt more doubt of myself. The only mass murderer who ever remained unidentified was Jack the Ripper and it looks as though there is a considerable similarity of action and motive. I frankly don't see what use I can be. But I've got to try."

"To that I can only say God Speed," said Mr. Gorringer and dismissed Carolus with a headmasterly gesture.

Four

CAROLUS had never been to Albert Park and his first impressions of it were damping. Just the sort of district, he reflected, for some dirty little schizo to let himself go with a butcher's knife, just the district to breed hatred, egomania, evil-mindedness, all the things that went to this sort of murder. The streets were unrelievedly ugly and even the houses overlooking the scrubby little park were heavy and pretentious like the people for whom they were built.

Albert Park had neither the honest rowdiness of Lewisham nor the still faintly eighteenth century gentility of Blackheath. Its houses were grim, built on basements to teach servants their place, ponderous without being grand, and the streets between them, labelled with important-sounding names, were almost deserted. There had been Spring in the air as he drove up from Newminster, but here there was not the faintest promise of Spring and it seemed that there never would be.

He went first to Salisbury Gardens, a long row of

double-fronted houses from behind whose lace curtains he could imagine leprous faces peering. He did not look out at Number 31, the Pressley home, or the house opposite, but turned his car at the top and made for Crabtree Avenue. It was nearly 5 o'clock and he thought if he reached St. Olave's Ladies College when the girls were leaving it, he might have a chance of seeing Miss Cratchley. He knew that tomorrow was the school's Breaking-Up day.

His car seemed to attract some attention as he drove it in the school gates and made for a square of asphalt on which two cars were already standing. He had barely switched off his engine when a middle-aged man in overalls approached him.

"No cars allowed in here," he said, but dubiously. "What are you, a parent?"

"No. I want to see Miss Cratchley."

"Oh, Press," said the man understandingly. "Well, I wonder how *you'll* get on. She's had most of them out before they've had time to turn round."

"Are you the caretaker?"

"S'right. Well, night watchman would be more like it, specially since we've had all this with the murders. Oh, thank you very much, Sir. Only don't let her see your car here or you'll get me the sack. She's hot on cars coming in."

"Where will I find Miss Cratchley?"

"I could show you where her study is but don't go and tell her I done it."

"You seem rather scared of the headmistress."

"Wait till you see her. That's all. It's not the job I worry about, specially now the missus daren't put her face outside the gates for fear of the Stabber. But I hate trouble of any sort. Easy come, easy go. That's me.

Come on, this way. I'll just show you which door it is then I shall have to hop it. She's usually there at this time in case there's anything to clear up. That's her car, see? Now, down that corridor, round to the left and the first on your left. And good luck."

Carolus knocked boldly.

"In," replied a quick voice.

He found himself facing a handsome grey-haired woman, not sitting like a business magnate at her desk but upright in an armchair with a tea-tray beside her. She showed no surprise but said "Who are you?" steadily as she scrutinized him.

Carolus decided to take a chance.

"Shake you if I said I was the Stabber, wouldn't it?" he said fatuously.

"Not in the least. What do you want?"

"One or two details about Hester Starkey."

"I thought I'd finished with the Press weeks ago." She rose and moved to ring a bell.

"I'm not Press."

"Well, you're not Police, are you? I've finished with them, too."

"No. I'm a schoolmaster."

"Good gracious. What on earth can a schoolmaster want with details about poor Starkey. Did you know her?"

Carolus shook his head.

"It's worse than that. Worse than if I wanted to sell you a vacuum-cleaner. I'm a private investigator."

A frosty smile appeared for a moment.

"I see. And you think *you're* going to discover this murderer, do you?"

"I can try."

"What makes you suppose you might?"

Carolus answered that with a question.

"Have you lost many girls through this?"

"Surprisingly few, so far. We take them out in a crocodile in the afternoon, and send them down Cromarty Avenue. The police have been very helpful and put two men on when the girls are coming in or going out. But I fear our numbers will be down next term unless this is cleared up. Sit down Mr. . . ."

"Deene. Carolus Deene. May I ask you my questions?"

"If they're not too ridiculous. It's no good poking about in poor Starkey's private life. That will tell you nothing about the murderer."

"Yet that's just what I'm going to do. Investigate each of these murders separately as though they were unconnected."

"But they were not unconnected. A child could see that."

"Perhaps not. But that's my line of approach. And it might work."

"What do you want to know?"

"Anything you care to tell me about her."

Miss Cratchley smiled.

"Tall order. She wasn't a bitter woman, if that's what you think. So many people imagine that this profession makes women bitter. She was alive and interested in many things. Pictures, books. She edited the school magazine."

"Was she popular?"

"With the girls? She was respected. She did not encourage girls to lose their heads over her. She taught well and was a good disciplinarian. I miss her a great deal."

"Did you like her, Miss Cratchley?"

"What a very odd question. No, I don't think I did, particularly. I valued her help."

"Had she any money beyond her salary?"

"I shouldn't think so. There was a rich relative somewhere, I believe."

"Had she many friends?"

"Outside the school I know of none. But then I wouldn't. I leave my staff severely alone in their own time. In the school she had two—of a sort. I suppose her friend, perhaps her only real friend, was another mistress here, Gerda Munshall. But there was also, in a way, the games mistress Grace Buller."

"In a way?"

"Oh, Grace is a big sentimental woman who loves everyone and can't bear it when someone doesn't love her. Gerda Munshall's a very different type. Highly intelligent. Perhaps a little too much emotion—repressed and otherwise. She, I think, was devoted to Hester Starkey."

"Do you mind if I talk to these two?"

"Wait till after tomorrow, will you? They'll be on holiday then, after this *very* difficult term. I'll give you their addresses. I don't know why I feel a certain confidence in you, Mr. Deene, but I do."

"Thank you. Yes, it must have been a trying time for you."

"Trying? You're a schoolmaster, you tell me. Try to imagine what it's like to have a murder in a school. A sensational murder such as this. I must say the parents have acted splendidly, most of them. I immediately called a parents meeting and addressed it. I'm pleased to say I seem to have their confidence. But it's a grave responsibility, Mr. Deene. That's why I catch at any straw."

"Even me."

"Just so. Leave me your address in case I need to get in touch with you again."

"I'm in rather a difficulty there. I usually stay in the town when I'm investigating. But somehow, Albert Park . . ."

"Exactly. I quite understand. Have you a car?"

"Yes."

"Then stay at the Golden Cockerel Guest House. Ten miles out in quite pleasant country. It's good. Professionally run. Comfortable. You'll like it. I shall phone you there if I want to see you."

His life for the next week or two thus ordered by Miss Cratchley, with no chance of forming any preferences of his own, Carolus rose to take his leave.

"I have to see the Detective Superintendent in charge of the case," observed Miss Cratchley. "He's coming here at six o'clock. I'm afraid I don't expect any good news. Perhaps you'll be able to bring me some soon. Good night."

Waiting about outside was the man in overalls.

"*You've* done it," he said. "The others was out on their ears in no time. She's a terror, isn't she? Tell you what you wanted to know, did she?"

"Yes, thanks."

"There's one of them that's had her picture in the papers still here if you want to catch her before she goes. Miss Buller, it is. The games mistress. She's down in the bike shed trying to start her motor-scooter, *as* usual. Want a word with her? This way then."

Grace Buller was perspiring.

"Oh Titchcock," she said to the caretaker. "*Can* you start my engine? You did the other night."

"I'll see what I can do. There's a gentleman here from the newspapers wants a word with you."

"Oh! Hullo! I'm afraid I'm in rather a state. Are you from the *Daily Post?*"

"No. I'm not a pressman. But I do want to ask you a few questions about Hester Starkey."

"You do? What for? You're not the police."

"I've just seen Miss Cratchley. I'm trying to be of some assistance. Did you have the same trouble with your engine on the night Hester Starkey was murdered?"

"Yes. That's the awful thing. If it had started at once I might have been there to save her. I still can't bear to think of it. And we'd quarrelled, you know."

"Yes. What about?"

"Nothing, really. That's what makes it all so dreadful. It was just that during the Break that morning . . . well, she always had a chat with me in the Break. I wanted to tell her something rather funny one of the girls had said. I went to the staff common-room as usual and poured out her coffee as I always do and took it over to the two chairs in the corner where we sit. *Our* chairs I always called them. And she never came in. I waited the whole half hour. Afterwards I heard she'd been up in . . . one of the classrooms."

"Which one?"

"Gerda Munshall's, as a matter of fact. She's the French mistress."

"A great friend of Hester's?"

"I suppose she was, sometimes. They had terrible quarrels though. Hester used to tell me about them. She liked to confide in me. It's dreadful to think she's . . . she's . . ."

"Yes, but it's rather foolish to blame yourself, Miss Buller."

"I know. But how can I help it? She was a wonderful person."

"Tell me about that evening. How long did it take you to get your engine started?"

"It seemed a long time. I told the police it was twenty minutes, but it may have been more."

"And when you came out at last there was no one in the avenue?"

"Not a soul. I can swear to that. I've been over it in my mind a thousand times. Do you think I wouldn't have noticed."

"Yes," said Carolus calmly.

"You mean, I mightn't have?"

"You had no reason to, that night."

"But looking back I should have. Knowing what I did then."

"Will you just think again, Miss Buller? Anything you might have noticed. For instance, did you pass a policeman?"

"A policeman? I should have noticed, wouldn't I?"

"Not necessarily. He would be part of the street, like Chesterton's postman."

"I'm sure I didn't. I'd have noticed. I always think I'm doing something wrong on the scooter. I haven't had it very long, you see. I'd have been wondering if he was going to stop me. No I'm sure I didn't. There wasn't anybody. I saw Mr. Slatter, of course . . ."

"Mr. *Who?*"

"Slatter. He's the park-keeper. He lives in the little lodge in the park. I see him almost every night as I go home."

"Have you just remembered this?"

"No, certainly not. I'm not a fool."

"You told the police?"

"About Mr. Slatter? Of course not. He's the park-keeper. Everyone knows him."

"Where was he?"

"Just going to his lodge, I suppose. Along Inverness Road. He'd probably been to the Mitre on the corner."

"But he could have been in Crabtree Avenue?"

"Mr. Slatter? Whatever for? He's a dear old man. Well not old, really. Anything else you want to know?"

"Did you know Hester's brother?"

"No. She never asked me to her home. I believe Gerda Munshall has been. You'd better ask her."

"Yes, I will."

"I don't know when you're going to see her, though. She'll be off to the Continent as soon as term's over tomorrow. At least she always *was*, with Hester. She has private money, you see, and could afford to invite Hester. Well, not invite her exactly but I'm sure she paid more than half of everything. They wouldn't tell *me* that, of course."

"I think the caretaker has got your scooter started."

"Thank heavens. Now I shall be able to get home."

"Where's that, Miss Buller?"

"Greenwich. It takes me nearly an hour sometimes when the traffic's bad."

"What time did you get home on the night of . . ."

"Oh, I don't know. I didn't notice. Late, anyway."

"Thank you, Miss Buller."

Carolus found the Golden Cockerel Guest House, a large Georgian place standing in the remains of its own ground, pleasantly situated and promising. He was shown a large room and told the terms, which were high. He had a bath and went down to the discreet little bar set in a corner of the lounge. No one was behind it but a bell-push was marked "Please Ring for Service" and brought a smart young waiter from the dining-room who gave him his whisky-and-soda. It all seemed well-organized and, as Miss Cratchley had said, professional.

While Carolus sat at the bar, a large man entered and walked purposefully across to him.

"Your name Deene?"

"Yes."

"I'm Superintendent Dyke. What the devil do you mean by questioning Miss Cratchley?"

"You'd better calm down a little," said Carolus amicably. "Have a drink?"

"It's a damned impertinence. I gather you're some kind of private investigator. You'd better understand that I won't have that kind of thing in a case of mine. What other police officers may have put up with I don't know, but I won't have it. You'd better get out of this place at once."

Carolus watched the man's puffy face and keen intelligent eyes, but did not answer.

"Haven't I enough to do keeping the blasted Press away? This isn't a case for amateur dabblers. It's a serious matter and I've got a heavy responsibility. I should have thought you might have the intelligence to see that."

"I do think you should have a drink," said Carolus.

"You'll leave this case alone, you understand? If I catch you hanging round or interfering with any of my witnesses I'll run you in for impeding the police in the execution of their duty. You're up against the wrong man this time, I can tell you. What d'you think you're up to, anyway? What's your object?"

"I? Oh, I'm just interested," said Carolus mildly but infuriatingly.

"Just interested, are you? Well, you'd better find something else for your interest. There's nothing for you in this."

"Well, now you've got that off your chest, may I repeat my invitation?"

"I don't want to drink with you. I've had amateur messers round a case before and they've never done anything but make difficulties."

"I've every sympathy. But just now and again, you know, one does hit on some little thing that's helpful. And I don't quite see how you can prevent me staying in this hotel and mooching round Albert Park during my school holidays."

"Maybe I can't. But let me catch you, just once, doing something that gives me a chance to run you in, and you've had it."

"Right. Now on *that* understanding?"

"I'll have a Scotch," said Dyke.

Carolus 'rang for service' and replenished his own glass while ordering Dyke a double.

"I only arrived today," said Carolus blandly. "But quite by chance a little thing did happen to fall into my lap, this evening. You probably know all about it from some other source."

It was Dyke's turn to say nothing but now his sharp hostile eyes watched Carolus.

"I had a talk to that games mistress," said Carolus and stopped, determined that the other should show some interest.

"Well?" said Dyke grudgingly.

"She *did* see someone that evening. Someone so much a part of the landscape that she never thought of mentioning him to you."

"In Crabtree Avenue?"

"Just round in Inverness Road I gather."

"Who was that?"

"So you don't know? Well, well. I don't suppose it has the least significance. It was the park-keeper, Slatter."

Carolus watched, and was rewarded. Dyke could not quite control his plump poker face.

"Slatter," he said, with something like a gasp, in that sound revealing that consciously or sub-consciously some suspicion had already entered his mind connected with Slatter.

"He was probably only going to the Mitre for a pint," Carolus pointed out.

Dyke pulled himself together.

"He probably was. And in any case, Deene, don't think for a moment that piece of information gives you the slightest status in this thing. I warn you again. Keep away from it or you'll find yourself in trouble. Serious trouble. I'm not a man to fool about. I mean what I say."

"Cheerio," said Carolus raising his glass, and Dyke gave a grunt.

Five

It was with some relief that Carolus had learned from Miss Cratchley that Gerda Munshall lived in London. He was beginning to feel the atmosphere of Albert Park seep into him like a damp mist and although this was part of his object in remaining there, or nearby, to *feel* that grim respectable suburb and know some of its people, he welcomed the chance to leave it for an evening.

He telephoned Gerda Munshall after dinner on that first night at the Golden Cockerel and she at once asked him to call on her next day.

"I shall be home soon after six and shan't go out again," said a sugary voice. "Tomorrow is our Breaking-Up day and I shall be dead beat. What time would you like to come?"

"Could I come early? Soon after you get in?"

He did not want to commit himself to taking Gerda out to dinner till he had met her, but he had this in mind.

"But certainly. Say six-thirty? You know the address?

Titan House, near Victoria Station. It's the twelfth floor, number 317."

He found Titan House—who could fail to?—and eventually the cell number he sought. His ring was answered by a tall dark sanguine woman with prominent eyes. "A little too much emotion," Miss Cratchley had said and he at once thought Gerda Munshall somewhat excessive in other ways—too much hair, too much make-up, too much scent and too much *manner*.

"*Do* come in," she said, "and forgive the pig-sty. You haven't left me time to put it straight. I just *snatched* a few daffodils from a stall because I can't *bear* to be without flowers but what it needs is a good old dusting. Helene told me you would call."

"Helene?"

"The Head. Hester and I *always* called her Helene, though not to her face, poor sweet. Can I give you a drink?"

She drank sherry, Carolus noticed, but kept whisky and put the bottle beside him with a siphon.

"Before we discuss the tragedy," went on Gerda, "may I say how *glad* I am that someone intelligent and sensitive is looking into it. I'm sure the police mean well but this is a complicated affair, don't you think? Some dreadful schizophrenic at work. It needs someone with imagination to see into the dark places of his mind. I shall never *rest* till he has been discovered."

"Revenge?"

"Oh *no!* How can one hope to be revenged on a madman? Hester herself would never have felt like that. She was the *least* vengeful person. She forgave *all* her enemies."

"She had enemies?"

Gerda stared at him a moment.

"Not particular enemies. But she was discriminating, you know. She *couldn't* suffer fools gladly. She had exquisite taste, in people as in everything else. She hated everything and everyone second rate and *banale*. This, of course, roused resentment at times."

"I daresay."

"That silly girl Buller for instance. I believe you met her last night? Poor clumsy wretch, there were times when she almost hated dear Hester. Sheer jealousy, I suppose. She could not bear to see Hester and me together. We had a very beautiful friendship, you see, something that could not be cheapened by the 'long littleness of life' or the attitude of uninteresting people."

"I see. Any others who could be said to hate Hester Starkey at times?"

"Well, Hester wasn't very tolerant. And she could speak her mind. One or two of the parents upset her at different times, and she wouldn't stand for that. Helene used to *shudder*. Only a week before her death she told one girl's father not to behave like an idiot. A Mr. Sutton. I'm telling you this to show what kind of person she was. She was proud, proud. She feared absolutely no one."

"Anyone else she talked to like that?"

A rich smile came to Gerda's too-full lips.

"Oh lots, I'm afraid. Even to me, once or twice, for we had our tiffs. But more often to men. She rather despised men, Mr. Deene."

"Oh, Did she know many?"

"She couldn't be bothered with them."

"You mean—if I may put it so crudely—she never had affairs?"

Gerda looked at him.

"Curious how men's minds run on that. You can

never *believe* that you are not the prime essentials of life. Hester was beautiful in her way, you know. I daresay she was run after at different times. But since we met, eight years ago, she has never thought of all that. A friendship like ours . . ."

"You think there may be men who resented this?"

"Probably. But when I say she could speak her mind to men, I mean the kind of men one comes up against in everyday life. You know, parents, policemen, odd contacts one makes when travelling . . . that sort of person."

"Anyone in particular?"

Gerda smiled again.

"There was a *ridiculous* incident in the park last summer. Hester had arranged to play tennis with some of the senior girls and some dreadful people from one of the avenues wanted the court. There is some sort of park-keeper and the silly man tried to interfere. You should have heard Hester. The girls told me afterwards that the people who wanted to play fled in *terror*. As for the man, I don't suppose he ever forgot it. He should have known better than to try to be cheeky to someone like Hester. She had such *dignity* when she was aroused. I've watched her handle French porters and waiters and people. Nothing spitfire about her. Just cold and dignified. I admired her tremendously."

"Yes, I see you did."

"You couldn't help it if you knew her."

"That must make her loss all the more tragic for you. It was a terrible way to die."

"Terrible. Yet there was something fine in the way she did not cry out or anything. I think I can see her walking down that avenue. She had a firm walk and held herself upright, like a soldier. Perhaps she heard this brute coming up behind her and scorned to run away. She died instantly, I'm told. That's something. She was very brave."

Carolus gave her a moment's silence after that, then said quietly—"And you're convinced, Miss Munshall, that it was a complete stranger?"

"How is one to tell with a schizophrenic? I understand that in these cases, in the really terrible homicidal cases, they may be absolutely normal most of the time. How can one tell?"

"I meant, you are convinced that it was not someone with a motive for killing Hester Starkey?"

"Of course! Who could have any motive? Besides, don't we *know* it was a madman? The two murders that have followed Hester's are enough to tell us that, surely. No one could have a motive in all three. The victims never knew one another and had nothing in common."

"That's true. But you see I'm tackling each murder independently. I may be wrong, but that's my way. Would you consider Hester's death as a single crime, and tell me if anything occurs to you."

"I did, we all did, consider it as a single crime at first. There was nothing. No motive we could possibly think of. Even then, before there were any more deaths, we decided it *must* be a madman."

"And Hester Starkey was chosen quite by chance, you think?"

"By a tragic chance, yes. He may have been waiting for weeks till he found a woman alone and no one in sight. He certainly chose the right place. That ghastly avenue! I can never bring myself to go down it again."

"You used to spend your holidays on the Continent together, I believe. Did you go by car?"

"No. Neither of us could drive. We were always meaning to learn but didn't."

Again Carolus paused.

"Do you know Hester's brother?"

"Eamon? Yes. What about him? You're not going to tell me you suspect him, are you?"

"No. He has a perfect alibi. I wondered if you could tell me anything about him. I'm going to see him presently at the theatre."

"He's weak and vain. If it had not been for him Hester and I would have been sharing a flat long ago and this might never have happened. But Hester considered him a responsibility and took it seriously. He's one of those people who simply can't *cope*, if you know what I mean. She had to look after him."

"I see. I'm most grateful for all you've told me, Miss Munshall. It must have been a strain for you."

"I don't know. I suppose I'm getting used to being without her now. We get used to everything in time, don't we? Or don't we? Good-night, Mr. Deene."

Were there tears in her eyes as she stood holding the front door open? Her eyes were so large and liquid that Carolus could not be sure.

It took him some time to find Eamon Starkey's place of work which was called the Crucible Theatre and had been made from a disused warehouse in one of the remote north-western suburbs. Its facade was lit with one green arc light and instead of playbills and photographs outside it had a single hoarding on which was "Exp 19: *The Gyrostat* by Hu Nic" in starkly simple lettering. The foyer was ornamented with Europeanized African masks, curiously sophisticated and hideous versions of their primitive prototypes. The play was proceeding inside and the box-office and foyer were empty except for a young man in a scarlet shirt with a thin sad beard.

"Is there such a thing as a stage door?" asked Carolus.

"An interesting question," said the young man condescendingly. "Perhaps your name is Johnny?"

"No. I want to see a man called Starkey."

"We don't use names for the cast. Eam Star is Index Eleven."

"Oh, Where could I see him?"

"Nowhere, really, till after the Black."

"The Black?"

"We don't have curtains."

"You mean, till the play is finished?"

"It's not a play. That's the whole point. We've got away from all that."

"Well, the performance."

"Still less is it a performance. It is Mutual Consciousness."

"Till after the Mutual Consciousness is finished then? What time will that be?"

"We have no fixed time. It's the ruin of spontaneity. It depends on Index Two. Sometimes he takes half an hour over his third Visual Impact, sometimes only five minutes. Would you like to wait inside? There's plenty of room."

Human curiosity made Carolus accept and the young man, who spelt out his name Hy Nox, led him through a door into a strange barn-like room in which the movable chairs were arranged in groups, or pairs, or singly, as the audience desired.

"No stage," explained Hy Nox, scarcely to the surprise of Carolus, "just the two bemas."

Carolus saw that where one would expect to see the stage-boxes there was, on each side of the far wall, a semi-circular construction, on which figures were visible.

These were masked and clad in somewhat Greek attire and seemed to be proceeding in competition, those on the left bema apparently unaware of those on the right, so that a loud jumble of words was audible.

"To tell you the truth," said Hy Nox, "I find *The Gyrostat* a bit corny. All that Greek drag. It gives a wrong impression."

"Has Starkey . . . Index Eleven, a large part?"

Hy Nox looked pained.

"We don't have parts. Exegeses."

"I see. Has Index Eleven a large exegesis?"

"Highly significant. Two quadruple reiterations. That's the method we use to give emphasis. He says 'Live, live, live, live,' in Execution One, and 'Die, die, die, die,' before the last Black."

"Is that all?"

"All? It's an important Exegesis."

"He wears a mask, of course?"

"Of course. All indexes in *The Gyrostat* are masked."

"Does he use his natural voice?"

Hy Nox smiled.

"You're very naif," he said. "You don't seem to be at all in touch with the modern movement. He speaks as he feels, of course. It may be almost a lion's roar or a tired murmur. That's why every Mutual Consciousness is different."

"Why not have the stage . . . stages . . . bemas at the *back* of the auditorium?" suggested Carolus. "So that the play . . . the Mutual Consciousness proceeded behind the audience?"

"We did think of it," said Hy Nox, "but it wouldn't work here. The audience—you've no idea how bourgeois they are—would simply turn their chairs round and the whole effect would be lost."

"Can I buy a programme?" asked Carolus, feeling pretty bourgeois himself.

"Certainly," said Hy Nox and handed him a single sheet on which was a reproduction of a painting by Francis Bacon. "Index Three's being terse tonight," he observed. "I think it'll be over before half past ten." Then added unexpectedly—"We like to get round to the Wheatsheaf before it closes, when we can."

"Do you think I might wait for Starkey—I mean Index Eleven—round there? I'm dying for a drink, you see."

"Yes," said the young man huffily, "but you'll miss the big Interloc between Indexes Eight and Five. It's the best thing they've done so far."

"Another night, perhaps?" suggested Carolus. "You know what it is when one wants a drink? Most interesting, I'm sure."

"Next week we've got *Oedipus Limbo* on again. It's the most neoteric thing we've done."

"I mustn't miss that," said Carolus, "but just now, if you don't mind . . ."

"Very well. I'll tell Index Eleven. Who shall I say wants him?"

Carolus had an inspiration.

"C-a-r D-e-e," he spelt out and left Hy Nox looking a little happier.

But Eamon Starkey, when he reached the Wheatsheaf later, was something of a disappointment. A rather ordinary-looking man in his early forties, he wore conventional clothes and talked in a tiresomely refined voice.

"I wonder if you'd mind telling me a little about your sister," Carolus said when drinks were bought and Carolus had explained himself as tactfully as possible.

"I suppose so," said Starkey wearily. "To tell you the truth I'm getting a little bored with the whole subject. I was quite fond of my sister, but to find oneself involved in a sensational murder case is not funny."

"Involved?"

"What else could you call it? The press never stopped asking me questions. I might have been the murderer, the way they went on."

"Oh no," Carolus pointed out. "You had a cast-iron alibi."

"That, yes. I got to the theatre at six o'clock that evening and did not leave till about this time. But that hasn't stopped them asking questions. That man Dyke is a menace. Now what do you want to know?"

"Rather an odd thing, really. When you first heard of your sister's death, before anyone knew it was one of several murders, what did you think about it? Had you any suspicions at all?"

"Suspicions? Do you mean of anyone in particular?"

"Yes."

"Not really. I suppose if I thought anything at all it was that . . . well, something to do with that school, I suppose. All those terrifying women. Poor Hester wasn't popular, you know."

"I see. Anyone in particular?"

"I didn't know them well enough. I met that appalling Munshall once or twice. Capable of anything, I should have thought. But all that's been wiped out, hasn't it, by the other murders? If anyone at the school *could* have been suspected—and I don't seriously see how they could—they were certainly out of it when the other murders happened, weren't they?"

"That's the general and I must say quite logical view. Tell me, had your sister any men friends?"

Eamon Starkey smiled in a rather superior way.

"Hester? Surely you must have realized that she and that appalling Munshall spent *all* their time together and thought men altogether inferior beings?"

"That doesn't quite answer my question."

"No, I don't think she had. Unless you count old Scatton."

"I have never heard of him."

"I don't expect you have. He's our solicitor. Known us since we were children. Father's executor. All that sort of thing. He's a bachelor and I suppose in his funny old way been in love with Hester all his life."

"Where does he live?"

"Blackheath. Owns a lot of property there. Our flat belongs to him, as a matter of fact. That's why we lived there."

"You say 'old' Scatton. How old is he?"

"Oh, not decrepit. Sixtyish, I should say."

"Did your sister see much of him?"

"Mmm. Fair amount."

"Do you know whether he had ever proposed to her?"

"Oh yes. Often in the old days. I think once, years ago, they nearly got married, but it all blew over. Hester was a great one for what she called her freedom."

"One other thing, Mr. Starkey. I hope you won't think me impertinent but I am trying to work on this thing in my own way. What were your sister's financial circumstances?"

"She had none. Just her salary. Munshall has money, I believe, and of course old Scatton's a rich man. But Hester didn't worry about money."

"Had she any expectations?"

"If you could call it that. There's an old great-aunt

down at Bournemouth with a good deal of money. We were about the only relatives she had. But we didn't count on anything. It will probably all go to a dog's home."

"Thank you."

"I think you're wasting your time," observed Eamon. "I don't mind answering questions but I can't see the point in them. Poor Hester was just a chance victim. How does it help you to know all this about her?"

"Perhaps not at all. On the other hand . . ."

"Better if you could find out who the murderer is before he can do any more damage."

"Yes. Much better," agreed Carolus seriously. "I must really see what I can do about it. Are you still living at Blackheath?"

"I've still got the flat there. I nearly always stay with a friend in town while I'm working."

"Yes. Must be a long way out. How do you travel when you do go?"

"I have a motor-bike. Surprising, isn't it, for an actor? Like those nuns you see on motor-bikes in France. But I got a taste for the things during the war and really rather enjoy it."

"I can quite understand that. If you tell me you're enjoying working as Index Eleven I should find it more baffling."

"Well, it's work. There's money behind the Crucible."

"How long has your present show been running?"

"Oh, months. It had such a press, you see. Ken Tynan raved. But it's coming off now."

"Did your sister see it?"

"Yes. Came to the first night. She didn't say much but I think she was rather impressed. She came with Munshall."

"I'm most grateful for all your information, Mr. Starkey."

"Not Mr. Starkey here," said Hester's brother smiling, "Eam Star."

"Anyway, thank you. I think there are some . . . Indexes behind you who seem to expect you to join them so I'll run along."

Six

WHILE Carolus was at the Crucible Theatre that evening there was a violent quarrel between Mrs. Whitehill and her niece Viola at number 10 Crabtree Avenue, a quarrel which led to yet another public incident.

Viola was twenty-seven, a moderately nice-looking girl, a little too eager in manner and lacking natural charm. She wanted a husband and had been disappointed several times, till a discontented droop began to appear at the lips of her mouth and her eyes had a look of anxiety and strain which made her less attractive. Her parents had been killed in a plane crash when she was fifteen and the Whitehills had adopted her in a businesslike way as though moved by conscience rather than inclination. Stella Whitehill had a temper, but only once or twice during the twelve years of Viola's stay with them had shown any impatience with the girl.

But it was not an altogether happy situation. Viola was useful to her aunt in the house and so had not been encouraged to seek employment, but not so useful that

Stella Whitehill wanted to keep her from marriage. On the contrary aunt and niece were united only in their wish to find a husband for Viola. It was a somewhat old-fashioned situation but nonetheless real to the two women who never discussed it except obliquely.

Stella Whitehill was short and heavy, yet gave an impression of power as though she had a powerful bony frame under folds of flesh. She had dark quick eyes and wore too much jewelry and her husband feared her. She was not an unkind woman and had tried in a way to do what she felt was her duty towards Viola, but on that evening her reserves fell away and she became an angry primitive who wanted her cave to herself. Perhaps in the stress of events in Crabtree Avenue she had taken to a nip too many of the gin-and-peppermint she liked, perhaps it was a natural fit of exasperation. At all events she spoke outrageously to Viola.

It was about Stanley Gates, who lived at the lower end of the avenue with his parents. This pleasant pink-faced insurance agent had spoken several times to Viola of late on affairs of the avenue, and this evening, an unusually warm one for March, they had walked through the park together. Stella Whitehill, hearing of this from Viola, said unforgivably—"Well, this time, for goodness sake don't try to rush him."

Viola, flushing furiously, asked "What do you mean 'this time'?"

"You know very well what I mean. Give the man a chance to breathe."

"Aunt Stella you . . ."

"Don't say it, because you'd be sorry afterwards. I'm only talking for your own good."

"You're being beastly. I don't 'rush' people."

"What about that Captain Greaves? And that poor

fellow at Sidmouth? You'll never get a man if you don't show some restraint."

"How *can* you talk like that? I've never . . ."

"Oh yes, you have. And you know it. It's time I told you this. I've watched it over and over again. You behave as though you were desperate. If you are, for God's sake don't show it, Viola. It scares a man. It scares me, for that matter."

Viola just managed not to cry.

"It's all lies," she said a little hysterically. "Stanley told me this evening . . ."

"Who is Stanley?"

"Stanley Gates. He told me this evening that I was one of the most reserved people he had ever met."

Stella gave a nasty chuckle.

"It's not a question of reserve. I'm not saying you're not reserved in a way. It's something worse than that. You show your cards. You as good as say you're twenty-seven and unlucky. Not by lack of reserve."

"How, then?"

"I don't know. It's something in your manner. Just give this man a chance to decide for himself."

"So that *you* won't have to go on keeping me, I suppose?"

If Viola expected reassuring denials she was disappointed.

"Well, there is that side of it," said Stella Whitehill. "I've never mentioned it before but naturally your uncle and I when you came to live with us thought it would be for five years or so . . ."

"Oh!" cried Viola and burst into tears.

"It had to be said, sooner or later," went on Stella philosophically.

"How *can* you?" cried Viola and grew somewhat

incoherent. "After all these years . . . slaving. I've never . . . Oh, you're cruel."

"Cruel to be kind," said Stella. "It's time you realized. We're getting on and the time comes when middle-aged people want to be on their own, have their home to themselves."

Viola stood up.

"You shall have your home to yourselves," she shouted. "Now. This minute. I'll go and take my things. Tonight. Now."

"Don't be silly, Viola. Where will you go?"

"I'll go to Stanley!"

"To Stanley? To young Gates? He lives with his parents."

"I don't care. I'm going to him."

"*That* would be the end of any chance you might have."

"How *dare* you talk like that?"

"But wouldn't it, Viola? To arrive on the doorstep. It's ridiculous."

"I'm going. I'm going," cried Viola and rushed from the room. A few minutes later Stella heard the front door slammed.

Viola with a small handbag, went to the gate and looked out. For the first time she remembered the murders in Crabtree Avenue.

It was a gusty night, but not too cold and there was no rain. She looked down the street and saw no one in sight, no police patrol, no Vigilantes, but on the other hand no single mysterious figure. The trees near St. Olave's Ladies' College waved their arms wildly and shadows seemed to be dancing everywhere. Should she return to the safety of her aunt's home? Her uncle would welcome her, at least, when he came in. But how could she face her aunt? She had shown the resolution to walk out, now she must go on.

After all it was not far. Down the avenue, just visible before it reached the better lighted Inverness Road, was number 52 where Stanley would be sitting with his parents. Stanley who had said that very afternoon that he wished he could have the chance to look after her. Just down there on the left. She would be there in five minutes.

She decided to walk in the middle of the road, neither on the pavement near the gardens of Crabtree Avenue, nor near the railings along the side of the park. Hadn't she heard that the . . . the Stabber was believed to have hidden in one of those gardens and stepped out behind his victim? Or, some said, come over the park railings. She would walk right in the centre.

Still no one was in sight. She saw several cars parked along the curb, but that was as usual. If only a policeman could have been walking up the street. Just one policeman. Or Stanley himself. How wonderful that would be. Stanley coming to meet her.

She was approaching the first of the parked cars, which was alone, a good many yards from the others. Suddenly she stopped, breathing heavily. For she saw, not very plainly but still beyond any hope of mistake, that in the driving seat was a man.

It seemed to Viola that she stood there a long time. She and the man must be glaring at one another though she could not see his eyes. Then she started to take paces backwards, not daring to turn. As she did so a terrifying thing happened. The door of the car began to open and a being emerged. She could not see the face but she was aware of glasses, a cloth cap and a raincoat.

She tried to scream, but no sound would come. She

opened her mouth wide, but all that emerged was a squeak from the back of her throat. Then as the man shut the door of his car and stepped towards her the scream came, long and piercing. She caught a blurred glimpse of the man getting back in his driving seat then the car was disappearing fast towards the lights of Inverness Road. She screamed again, then collapsed painfully on the pavement.

Half an hour later on the settee of her aunt's drawing-room to which she had been carried by scared neighbours, she was able to tell her story to one of Dyke's assistants. It was not without embellishments, none of which were conscious lies but had been added by hysterical double vision.

She had *seen*, for example, his red glaring eyes. Wasn't he wearing glasses? Yes, but she had seen them, under the peak of his cap, like a wild animal's eyes. And somewhere, she was not sure where or at what point, she was *sure* she had seen a blade. A long blade, like that of a butcher's knife. Was the man carrying it? She couldn't be certain. She had seen it, that was all she could say.

Had the man spoken to her? No. That was the awful part. That silence. It had gone on and on as he came crouching towards her. Crouching? That's what it seemed like. How many paces? She didn't know. He had been advancing on her for a long time while she couldn't scream. But where she had fallen was only seven yards from where the car stood. She couldn't tell that. It seemed ages, anyway.

The detective inspector examining Viola asked his next question with concealed suspense. He had some experience of hysteria and the curious contradictions of its victims.

"Did you notice the car, Miss Whitehill?"

"Oh yes. The man was sitting in it."

"Did you notice what make it was?"

"No. Not the make."

"What colour was it?"

"Black, I think."

"Sure it wasn't light grey?"

"It might have been."

"There was a green car standing there this evening."

"That was it. Green. Or was it blue? So hard to tell in that light."

"Was it large or small?"

"Not very large. Not a mini-minor, or anything tiny like that. Yes, fairly large, now I come to think of it. I saw the man through the windscreen. I knew at once who it was. I can see his eyes now . . ."

"But could you *then*, Miss Whitehill? There couldn't have been much light on him and you say he was wearing glasses."

"Yes, I'm sure he was wearing glasses. I saw them when he got out and started coming for me. I can't remember any more. I can't even remember twisting my ankle."

"That was when you fell down. Was the man coming for you then?"

"No, no," said Viola with sudden lucidity. "No. Not when I fell. He was getting back into the car then. I saw the car drive away, fast down the road."

"You didn't, of course, see anything of its number?"

"Oh no. It just went away. I can't tell you any more."

"One other thing, Miss Whitehill, while it's fresh in your memory. Was the man tall or short?"

Viola tried to think, but shook her head.

"Just ordinary, so far as I could tell."

"Had you ever seen him before?"

"No. I don't think so."

"Did he remind you of anyone?"

"Not at the time."

"Has he made you think of anyone, since?"

"A little, yes, of my father."

"Is your father living?"

"No. He died twelve years ago."

"Thank you, Miss Whitehill. If anything else occurs to you, you'll let us know, won't you?"

"I've told you everything."

The doctor arrived soon afterwards and gave her a tranquilizer. But Viola, as her aunt said crisply, was never quite the same again. She had fits of vacancy and had to give up Bridge-playing because she could not concentrate.

"A tragic thing," said Stella Whitehill, and for her and her husband it was.

It was not even of much help to the investigation. It was quite possible, as Dyke had at once realized, that the stranger in the car was a normal citizen waiting for someone to join him from the house outside which he was parked. This was Number 28, and questioning of its occupants, the Turnwrights, and those of the neighbouring houses, revealed nothing. But the man could have been quite harmless and when he started to get out it could have been to reassure Viola when he saw her stop in the road. The glaring eyes and the knife could be the result of hysteria, the crouching approach was almost certainly this. As for the man's quick retreat—the most harmless person, knowing what had been happening in Crabtree Avenue, might have done what the man did. Finding himself screamed at by a young woman he could easily have fled before the neighbours came out of their houses.

On the other hand it could, of course, have been the Stabber, scared away at the last moment by that piercing scream, the first uttered by one of his victims. If it was, a car may have been used in the other cases and the Stabber have come from a considerable distance. It was all hypothesis and speculation.

Carolus heard nothing about it that evening when he returned from the Crucible Theatre and had to gain his knowledge next day from newspaper reports. These were lurid in the extreme and according to one the butcher's knife was actually raised above the girl when neighbours, hearing her screams, had come to her rescue. Carolus decided to be content with what he read rather than attempt to see Viola for the present. The hostility of Dyke and his own lack of status in the whole affair made it difficult for him to do any more than wait and hope that presently he might have an opportunity of meeting the Whitehills and their niece and asking his own kind of seemingly innocent questions.

In fact, he found this case exhausting and decided to return to Newminster for the week-end. The method he had chosen seemed to him to give some hopes, but it would be a lengthy process for he yet had to examine the circumstances surrounding the deaths of Joyce Ribbing and Mrs. Crabbett.

It was a relief to come from the murky respectability of those Hibernian-titled avenues to his own quiet house and be among familiar objects. But when Mrs. Stick brought in his bottle and siphon on a scrupulously polished tray, he saw at once that he was under suspicion.

"It's to be hoped you've been having a nice holiday, Sir," she observed with a note of enquiry.

"Splendid, thank you, Mrs. Stick."

"Perhaps you've been down at the seaside."

"No. No. Not the seaside this time."

"We *did* hear, though I'm sure we didn't wish to believe it, in spite of someone telling us straight out, that you'd been up to that Albert Park where all the murders are. I was only saying to Stick, I don't believe it, I said. Mr. Deene would never get himself mixed up with anything as nasty as that, not after all he's said in the past. Because if he was to, I said to Stick, we should have to go, that's all. We couldn't have another upset like that last one, when we never knew from one day to the next whether you wouldn't be banged over the head with a hammer."

"Yes, that was an unpleasant affair, wasn't it, Mrs. Stick?"

The little woman watched Carolus through her steel-rimmed glasses.

"It's not for me to ask questions, Sir," she said. "But with my sister already half thinking we oughtn't to be where we are, with all these murders and that, I must go so far as to say that we couldn't have another. We should have to give our notice. But lets hope they were telling us wrong about Albert Park."

"What have we got for dinner, Mrs. Stick?"

"Well, I thought you might like it for a change, Sir. I'm going to do some brochits. Shooshky babs, they call them. Over charcoal, which I got in specially. Then there's some cream fright afterwards."

Carolus stared for a moment.

"*Crème Frite*," he gasped as understanding dawned. "Excellent, Mrs. Stick."

Seven

WHEN Carolus reached Albert Park next morning he drove straight to Dr. Ribbing's house and asked for him. He was received by a smiling little man.

"I'm Ribbing's *locum*," he explained. "Poor chap has been sent away for a holiday. He broke down altogether, you know."

"Sorry to hear that. Can you tell me where I can find him?"

"No. I certainly cannot. If you're a patient of his I'll see you."

"I'm not a patient," Carolus explained. "It was a personal matter."

"It will have to wait for his return in about a week's time, then. I can't give his whereabouts to anyone."

Carolus, thinking this over at the Golden Cockerel, decided that it was not a serious setback. There was no reason why he should, in his casual-seeming investigations, follow the same order as the murderer. He would look into the death of Mrs. Crabbett first and when Ribbing returned, tackle the other case.

His first interview must clearly be with the widower, and he was grateful to the Press for the knowledge that Crabbett lived in Bromley and to the Telephone Directory for his address—Crabbett, James d'Avernon, 24 Bentink Hse, Maidstone Rd, Bromley. He set out to chance finding his man at home.

Crabbett was of medium height, a modest-looking man in his fifties with a rather shy smile. To make opening conversation, Carolus said he knew some d'Avernons and wondered whether they were relations. This seemed rather to embarrass Crabbett.

"To tell you the truth that is not my name," he said. "The wife had an aunt who became a Mrs. d'Avernon and she took a fancy to the name. She liked to be addressed as d'Avernon Crabbett. Her first name was Hermione so it made a bit of a mouthful. Harmless, really. I didn't mind."

Carolus carefully explained why he had called, pretending to no official status and apologizing for troubling Crabbett.

"Oh, that's all right. It's a relief to talk about it. The police did not seem to understand how I felt and the Press were terrible. I should like to give you any help I can. I don't want others to suffer."

"That's kind of you. Am I to gather from what you tell me of your wife's name that she took that sort of thing rather seriously?"

"You mean, was she a snob? I daresay some people thought so, but they did not know her kind nature underneath it. My wife was well-to-do, Mr. Deene, and very generous. She supported many local charities."

"You speak as though it was *she* who did all the good work."

Crabbett looked rather bashful, almost boyish.

"Well, we both did our best, of course."

"You are in business, Mr. Crabbett?"

"I retired a good many years ago. I was in shipping. There was no need for me to continue and my wife . . . we liked to be together. But I thought your questions would be about her tragic death."

"I like to get the background. You had only one daughter?"

"Yes. Isobel. It was to see her that my wife had gone on the night . . ."

"You have grandchildren?"

"Only one. A girl of three. But . . ."

"Your wife went often to see your daughter?"

"Oh yes. Every Thursday. And they came here of course. They . . . we . . . were all good friends. Very good. I don't always see eye to eye with my son-in-law but I've no doubt he's an excellent fellow. Harry Pressley. He works for a firm selling hearing-aids and similar appliances."

"You didn't accompany your wife?"

"Not that evening. I drove her over as I always do and arranged to call for her at seven."

"Was that your usual time for fetching her?"

"No. It was usually eight. She wanted to be earlier that night to see a programme on the telly. I feel responsible for her death you know, Mr. Deene. I'm inclined to be vague and it must have been nearly eight when I reached the house. I had come back here, you see, and was lost in a crossword puzzle. *The Times*, in fact. Perhaps you're addicted to crosswords?"

"I am indeed. Have you finished today's? That one across 'South to the Cape, winter woollies discarded' . . ."

Crabbett became animated.

" 'Shorn', of course," he cried. "The only one I couldn't do was 'Further outlook 4, 4' ".

" 'Long view' " supplied Carolus. "Funny how you can stare at them, isn't it? And how easy they look afterwards."

"I know. You can understand, then, how I came to be late in fetching my wife? Besides there was the fact that my usual time for picking her up was eight. Still, I blame myself terribly for it."

"But you weren't very late. I should have thought she would have waited for you?"

"You didn't know her," said Crabbett, almost smiling. "She was so punctual herself always. My daughter said she phoned here before she left and got no answer."

"But wouldn't that have suggested you were on your way?"

"Not to Hermione, I fear. She would return by Blue Line. Quite an easy journey and she knew a bus left at 7:55. No, there is really no excuse for me. I ought to have been there. Especially after those two murders in Crabtree Avenue, quite nearby. It was known there was some kind of maniac at large. If I had left home only a quarter of an hour earlier I should have saved her. You must forgive me for repeating that but it's very much on my conscience."

"I don't see why it should be. There are many 'ifs' by which you might have prevented the crime. If you had gone with her to see your daughter, for instance."

Crabbett blinked mildly.

"Yes, of course. That would have done it, wouldn't it? Only she particularly wanted to go alone that day. Women *do* like a chance for a chat between themselves.

I always let them have it. You're not married, Mr. Deene?"

"No. But I can understand that. Have you a photograph of your wife that I could see?"

"Of course I have. Several. I'll go and get one."

He returned with a large photograph in an ornate silver frame which matched several other frames on an occasional table. Carolus looked into the strong face of a rather handsome woman elaborately dressed.

"Taken some years ago," said Crabbett. "She was a good-looking woman, don't you think?"

He was interrupted by dog noises in the other room.

"Do you mind?" he asked Carolus, and released a spaniel puppy which began to coil and lick and generally demand attention. Carolus reached out a hand to the little creature to be smothered with wet kisses.

"Had her long?" he asked.

"It's a he. I call him Dover—my home town, you see. He's only been mine a few days though I've known his family for some time. They live downstairs."

"I'm surprised you can keep dogs in these flats."

"Oh it wasn't that. There's never been a rule against it." He paused then said in his shy manner—"I've been a bit lonely here since . . . it happened."

"I expect you have. You're quite alone? No domestic help?"

"Oh no," said Crabbett smiling again. "I don't need any. There's nothing I can't do in a house, from cooking to turning out a room."

"Lucky man. I wish I could. It must give you a wonderful sense of independence."

"Independence? Oh, I see. Yes. I haven't offered you a drink, by the way. May I?"

"Thanks. That's a neat little cabinet."

"Like it?" Crabbett seemed delighted. "I found it in a furniture shop yesterday. I think it's rather neat."

"You've certainly stocked it. May I have some of that dry sherry?"

They drank together.

"If you want to ask me any more about that evening," said Crabbett, "please don't feel diffident about it. I've gone over it so often now that I don't mind discussing it."

"Right. Then I'll fill in my picture. How long did you stay at your daughter's?"

"Oh, only a few moments. She told me Hermione had been gone about ten minutes and I said I would hurry back to get in before she reached home. I did that, but of course Hermione did not come."

"How soon did you start to worry?"

"Well, quite soon, really. As soon as I realized she couldn't have been on the bus. I couldn't think where else she could have gone. We don't know anyone in Albert Park except my daughter and her family. Then I thought she might have decided to make a call here in Bromley and rang up two friends of hers, a Mrs. Sticer and a family named Vogelman. Neither had seen her. By now it was well past nine."

"So?"

"Then Isobel phoned to ask if Hermione was in and when I said she hadn't come yet she got rather excited and began talking about the murders in Crabtree Avenue and said I must call the police. Do you know, Mr. Deene, I simply hadn't thought of those murders till then. It seems odd now, but at the time they never occurred to me. When Hermione did not come I thought of all sorts of things, accidents, illness, even some sudden impulse to go somewhere else, but I never thought of those murders. You see, I don't read much about that sort of thing and don't go out a lot. I hadn't heard them discussed as other people had. So when Isobel began talking about them it occurred to me for the first time that something like that might have happened. So I phoned the police at once. You know what they found."

"Yes. You've been most explicit, Mr. Crabbett. Now I have a suggestion to make. I would like to go over to Salisbury Gardens and have a chat with your daughter and son-in-law. Also to go over the ground, as it were. If it wouldn't be too painful for you, would you come with me? We could get some lunch first. I suppose there's somewhere in Bromley?"

"Oh yes. We could. As for going with you to Salisbury Gardens I'll certainly show you where it happened but I'll leave you to call on my daughter alone. I think she will tell you more if I'm not there."

"Just as you like."

"I must just feed Dover, if you'll hold on a minute."

Over lunch Carolus confided in Crabbett a few of the conclusions or half-conclusions he was drawing.

"I haven't asked any questions about the second murder," he said, "but I know something about the first. It has been said that the victims had nothing in common, but that's not quite true. All three, for instance, were small women, or at least short in stature."

"So they were," said Crabbett. "Does that indicate anything?"

"It suggests, but doesn't really indicate. The murderer might have had a grudge against small women. Or he might have been a small man himself, incapable of that particular knife-stroke on someone tall."

"Hermione was not remarkably short," said Crabbett. "I mean, no one would call her that. Just under the average, that's all. What else had they in common?"

"Well, your wife and Hester Starkey were both women of character."

"Hermione was that, I suppose. What else?"

"Nothing, that occurs to me. Your wife wasn't acquainted with either of the others, was she?"

"Not that I know of."

"No. There are no links between the three murders—except the murderer."

"What were you looking for? A common motive?"

"You can't discount motive," said Carolus defensively.

"Oh, I thought you could with a madman."

"Not even then," said Carolus.

They drove to the suburb of Albert Park in a few minutes and Crabbett suggested that Carolus should park his car some way from his daughter's house.

"I don't want her to see me or she'll wonder why I don't come in. Besides she has a very inquisitive neighbour, she tells me. She's rather sensitive about it. Anyhow, this is about opposite the garden in which Hermione was found. One of those."

"It was number 27," said Carolus.

"Then that's it. Just opposite."

"Yes, I see. So the murderer must have been waiting about here somewhere."

"I suppose so."

"May we walk down by the route that she would have taken to the bus-stop?"

"Certainly. It's not very far."

They reached the bottom of Salisbury Gardens and turned left along Inverness Road. In about twenty yards Oaktree Avenue, which ran up the west side of the park, turned off to their left and on its corner was the lodge gates. A man in uniform who was standing beside them greeted Crabbett.

"Afternoon, Mr. Crabbett," he called cheerfully.

Crabbett gave him a friendly reply and walked on.

"Slatter," he explained to Carolus. "The park-keeper. A very good chap."

"Known him long?"

"To tell you the truth I met him in the bar of the Mitre some months ago. The Mitre's on the next corner. I was waiting to pick up Hermione . . ."

"You'll forgive me asking this," said Carolus. "But did you *never* accompany your wife on her visits to your daughter?"

"Of course you can ask it. The answer is, not more often than I could help. I'm very fond of my daughter and little grandchild, but to tell you the truth I don't get on with Pressley. He's a self-opinionated fellow and in the end it came to an open dispute between us. That's why I scarcely ever went to the house."

"Of course. I see," said Carolus. Didn't he know these family situations?

"This is where Hermione would have taken the bus. So you see she hadn't very far to come on foot. I'm going from here myself."

"You've been very kind and helpful."

"Not a bit. Let me know if there's anything more I can do. I have a feeling you'll find your man, though."

Carolus rang the bell at Number 12, the Pressleys' home, and waited a long time for an answer. At last a woman with bright red hair and a toothy smile answered him.

"Oh yes," she said, "I've heard about you. Not supposed to tell you anything, are we? Or so I heard from one of the police. But I don't take any notice of them. Come in."

Carolus followed her into a drawing-room furnished with rather expensive modern pieces arranged with stereotyped good taste.

"You've seen my father, I suppose? Not that he could tell you much. Just like him to be late that night."

"Was it?"

"Dad? He's always late. Or has been for the last two years. Seems to have gone sort of dreamy though I can remember him when he was very wide awake. I'm sorry for him, really."

"Your mother's death was a tragedy for both of you."

"Oh, I didn't mean that. I meant—his life. He doesn't seem to take an interest in anything."

Carolus did not contradict this, though he had formed a very different impression.

"He has a dog to take an interest in now."

"A dog?" Isobel Pressley looked quite startled. "Has he really? Mother would turn in her grave. She couldn't bear dogs. Of course I don't see much of dad. He and my husband don't get on, really. They had a little difference some time ago and haven't spoken since. Dad's like that, very quiet and sort of shy, but, if he takes a dislike to someone he can't hide it. It made things very awkward sometimes. I suppose I get that from him, really."

Carolus turned the conversation back to more relevant matters.

"So when your father failed to come for your mother that evening it was nothing unusual?"

"I wouldn't say that. He'd never failed her like that before though he was often late. But we all knew dad."

"Your mother would not wait any longer?"

"No. I think she wanted to teach him a lesson. She knew he'd be very upset when he heard she'd had to go by bus."

"She was angry?"

"Well. Mother was a downright sort of person. When dad didn't come for her she just said 'I shall walk, then', and I couldn't persuade her. Though I must say we never thought of those murders at the time."

"Pity."

"Oh, I don't know. It wouldn't have made much difference, if I knew mother. If she'd made up her mind wild horses wouldn't change her, let alone the Stabber. She'd have gone just the same. We haven't a car or we'd have run her home."

"It was just before eight?"

"Yes, and he was supposed to have come at seven. You can't blame her for being a bit annoyed, can you? It isn't as though dad . . ."

"What were you going to say?"

"It's not very nice to talk about it, but it was mother who had the money. Dad retired ages ago, without much of a pension."

"Why did he do that?"

"Oh mother wanted him to. She had ideas for them, you see. Mother was always a bit . . . well, a bit *grande dame*, I suppose. It seems dreadful to say that now, but you know what I mean."

"I think so. I wonder whether I shall have an opportunity for a few words with your husband?"

"Harry. Why not? He can tell you more than I can. He's got a better memory. Only it's his late evening this evening. He'll be home quite early tomorrow. Why not come then? I suppose you're going to see that old bitch opposite? I thought so. You could call in afterwards, or before. She'll be dying to know who you are now. She'll guess you're not Press or police. Still. Never mind. You come in tomorrow and we'll tell you anything we can."

"Thanks. Your father tells me he sometimes has a drink at the Mitre so I suppose your husband uses another pub?"

"Well yes, he does when he has a drink which isn't very often. He goes to the King's Head. Mother was teetotal, by the way."

"Oh, was she?"

"I'm not, though. There were a lot of things mum was that I'm not, I'm afraid."

"Yet you all seem to have been very fond of her," pondered Carolus.

"Oh yes, we were. Even Harry, my husband, though he had his differences with her. I've known him swear he'll never be here again on a Thursday which was her evening for coming over. But he always got over it. Well, you couldn't help *liking* mum, even if she did put it on a bit."

"Thank you for all your information, Mrs. Pressley."

"I've told you nothing, really. But you come and see Harry tomorrow."

Eight

In one way this case differed from others which Carolus had tackled—here everyone was willing, and some were eager, to talk. It rather shook his confidence in his own method. Naturally since each of these women had been the chance-chosen innocent victim of a madman, their relatives had nothing to hide and were only too willing to chatter about Hester and her high-handed contempt for men or Hermione and her small-town grandeur, or doubtless, when he came to it, of Joyce and her idiosyncrasies. In most cases of murder there were connections between victim and murderer, between the circumstances and the act, which gave those left behind fears, anxieties and shames, and caused them to be evasive. Here everyone talked most willingly and generally, Carolus thought, truthfully.

Was it wrong then to apply his usual method of disingenuously questioning those connected with the victim? Was he wasting time? If so, if this case was to be his first failure, so be it. He could go about it no other way. The police with their resources and experience were able to attack by more direct methods, and perhaps the only ones that would succeed. They could use patrols, follow investigations of a well-organized kind, perhaps even use a policewoman out of uniform in an attempt to make the murderer break cover. For Carolus there was only his own time-honoured way—and the chance, by no means to be counted out—of a piece of luck. He must, he thought on the morning after he had seen Crabbett, bash on regardless, and his next inevitable interview must be with Miss Pilkin.

He waited, however, until the afternoon before ringing the bell of the house opposite the Pressleys'.

The door was opened by a bright young woman who called "Someone for you, Miss Pilkin," when Carolus had said what he wanted.

"I'll come down," called a voice from above.

"She'll be down in a minute," said the young woman unnecessarily. "She's just come in from her walk."

"Thank you."

"I better wait. She may not want to see you. She's had a lot come to call on her lately. She's very funny, you know."

"Funny?"

"You know what I mean. She's getting on. And living all alone like that. It's her house, really, only she lets us the ground floor and we look after her a bit. It's all that dog with her. Here she comes."

Miss Pilkin descended the stairs with some deliberation. She was a big bony woman with high cheek-bones and large weak eyes. Her clothes were untidy and she was festooned with beads and bangles.

"Gentleman to see you," said the young woman cheerfully.

"Turn to the light," Miss Pilkin commanded Carolus. "Let me see your face." She scrutinized him hungrily. "Ah yes, you have a good face. You may come up."

Carolus followed her to a Victorian sitting-room on the first floor where he was eyed incuriously by a Pomeranian dog lying on a cushion.

"Yes, Ursus approves of you, and he is a good judge of character. Please sit down and tell me what you wish to see me about."

Carolus introduced and explained himself, and asked if Miss Pilkin wished to say anything.

"I wish to say a great deal," she announced. "Things which I have said to no one. I have instincts in these matters, Mr. Deene, I have guidances, which are not to be ignored."

Carolus would have preferred facts, but nodded gravely.

"It may be you have, too. It may be that you have been guided to me. For I can help you."

"That's good. You know the people opposite, I believe?"

"I knew them, but I fear I always mistrusted them, or rather the man. I have acute perceptions in these matters and everything told me he was bad, bad. I was sorry for his wife and remained on friendly terms with her until she behaved with terrible cruelty to Ursus, my . . . I won't say my dog, for he is so much more than that, as you can see. My companion."

"How was that?"

"She was taking her child out in its wheelchair. I was on my way home from my afternoon walk with Ursus. It happens that he is devoted to children, a taste I do not altogether share. If he sees a child he likes to greet it. That is what he did on the afternoon I am recalling.

He went across to the wheelchair and said 'Good afternoon', as dogs do. As plain as could be, he was saying 'good afternoon' to the child, smiling at it, wanting to play, or perhaps be no more than polite. But the wretched child, instead of smiling and saying 'Good afternoon, Mr. Ursus' as any sensible child would, set up a howl, and the mother, this woman Pressley, began to belabour poor Ursus with an umbrella. It was not only from the blows he suffered. His feelings were hurt. To be struck and abused when all you have done is to be courteous and friendly was too much for him."

"Oh dear," said Carolus. "Yes. I see it all."

"I remonstrated, of course," continued Miss Pilkin. "Somewhat forcibly, in the circumstances. 'Don't you *dare* strike my dog!' I said. The woman's reply was unforgivable. She used language that would shame a costermonger. I could see this developing into a vulgar street-scene so I called Ursus and came in here, extremely angry. But that was not the end of the matter."

"No?"

"Not by any means. A few days later I was in the street alone on my way home from a meeting of the Theosophical Society when the man Pressley approached me. What he said I have written down because I subsequently complained to the police and did not care to use the words. You may, however, read them."

She fumbled in her bag and gave Carolus a worn piece of paper. On it he read "If your filthy, flea-bitten dog ever comes anywhere near my baby again I'll wring its bloody neck, and yours, too, you old bitch."

"So you see," said Miss Pilkin, "why I am no longer on speaking terms with these people."

"But you still know something of their movements?"

"I know everything of their movements. I have made

it my business to know. I owe it to Ursus to know. I have told the police a certain amount. I am prepared to tell you more, for you, I feel, will recognize that things are not just black or white, fact or fancy, but are subject to intuitions and perceptions such as mine."

"That night . . ."

"Long before that night, Mr. Deene, there had been trouble in this family. There had been angry disputes between Harry Pressley and Mrs. Crabbett . . ."

"*Mrs.* Crabbett?"

"Certainly. I have seen, nay heard, them shouting at one another in the most disgraceful way."

"What about?"

"Money, principally. There was a dispute on the night, on the very night of Mrs. Crabbett's death. I do not know the details. I heard nothing. But I *saw.* Pressley seemed to be threatening his mother-in-law with violence and then flung out of the house in disgust."

"At what time?"

"Half past six, I should say."

"And what time did he return?"

"It must have been nearly ten, and the worse for liquor. His walk was unsteady. When the police car first drew up at ten-thirty I wondered if he was sober enough to receive them. He must have been for it was he who opened the front door."

"Does he often go out at night like that?"

"I should not say often, but there are occasions."

"You have not, I suppose, taken note of the dates on which he has done so?"

"I have not. But there were other disputes, sometimes between Pressley and his wife. Sometimes between mother and daughter."

"More than with most families, would you think?"

"My father was a clergyman, Mr. Deene, and our home was free from bickering. I have no experience of such things. My good Mr. and Mrs. Wilson downstairs never have a cross word. These people opposite were for ever quarrelling."

"That is perhaps why Crabbett rarely accompanied his wife on her visits?"

"I cannot say. He would bring his wife in their car and stop a little way down the road."

"Why, I wonder?"

"I could only surmise that he did not wish to be involved in these family disturbances."

"You could see his car then?"

"Not always. But when Mrs. Crabbett walked up to the door I could observe it turning to drive away. Then later Mr. Crabbett would return for her."

"But not that last night?"

"Oh yes. But later than usual. He came to the front door and left almost at once. Evidently his daughter told him his wife had left."

"That was before Pressley's return?"

"Oh yes. Considerably. I was, of course, most upset to hear about Mrs. Crabbett. A terrible way to enter the Great Unknown. Far be it from me to wish ill to anyone, even to these unruly and cruel people. It was most distressing, particularly as I had seen the man who committed the crime."

"You saw him?"

"Oh yes. I told the police that. I saw him waiting about there."

"But how do you know . . . what makes you think it was the murderer?"

"Instinct, Mr. Deene. My instincts are infallible. The

man I saw in Salisbury Gardens that night was waiting to plunge a knife into a woman."

"You mean, you knew *at the time?*"

"Ah, if only it were as simple as that! In a sense I did so. I saw an aura of evil round him. I *felt* he was bad. But I did not foresee that within an hour he would have blood on his hands."

"He was a tall man?"

"No. He seemed to be of average height or perhaps a little smaller. But he was wearing a tall man's raincoat. It was visibly too large for him."

"You saw his face?"

"Not at all distinctly. I saw that he wore spectacles. His features were in the shadow of a cloth cap."

"Had you ever seen him before?"

"Not to recognize. Yet I was conscious of some sense of semi-recognition. Perhaps I had known him in a previous incarnation."

"You say he was waiting about?"

"That was the impression he gave. His hands were in the pockets of his raincoat. He disappeared more than once, up or down the road, into what shadowy places I know not. I saw him for the last time not long before Mrs. Crabbett emerged."

"Then did he disappear up or down the road?"

"Down. In the direction Mrs. Crabbett would take."

"That is all you saw?"

"I think so. Is it not enough? It is as though I saw that poor woman murdered before my eyes."

"Do you know many people in the district by sight, Miss Pilkin?"

"I believe I am as observant as most and I do not hold myself aloof. I gladly greet my fellows when I see them."

"Do you for instance know many from Crabtree Avenue on the other side of the park?"

"I knew the poor schoolmistress who was murdered, slightly. Some years ago, when I first decided to let part of my house, she came with her brother to view it. I also know some people called Goggins who are members of the Theosophical Society."

"Anyone else?"

"My good Mr. and Mrs. Wilson are related to the caretaker at St. Olave's Ladies College and have occasionally asked them here. I know no more."

"You take your dog in the park sometimes?"

"Daily. On a lead. Mr. Slatter insists on that, though the good fellow sometimes turns a blind eye when I give Ursus a little frolic on the lawn at the far end of the park."

"Thank you, Miss Pilkin. You have been most helpful."

A far-away look came into Miss Pilkin's bony face.

"Look for the murderer, Mr. Deene, in the faces of the dead women. They will tell you all. I had never to my knowledge seen the doctor's wife, but both of the others were hard, hard women, dominating women, bringing unhappiness to others."

"You don't think they were chosen by chance, then?"

"There is no such thing as chance and those we call insane are particularly sensitive to influences. They may be guided to acts of retribution. Cruelty can never go unpunished. The cruelty of one human being to another, continuing perhaps for years, is greater than the cruelty of a single blow. So I say look into the cruel and wicked faces of the dead and you will find the clue you want."

"Thank you."

"Study, also, the living," went on Miss Pilkin in the

voice of a prophetess. "Particularly those in the house opposite."

"Yes. I'm going there now," said Carolus.

"Remember then that every line in every face says something to him who understands. You *will* be successful. I see it in your eyes. Ursus, if he could speak, would say so too. But you mustn't let them hang the poor wild creature when you find him. He is under a compulsion such as you or I, thank God, can never imagine. He must be restrained, yes, but not hanged."

"He is a murderer," said Carolus.

"He is a madman," retorted Miss Pilkin, "and the Mohammedans say the mad are the children of God."

On that note Carolus left her and went to the house opposite. He found Isobel Pressley in a very different mood from yesterday.

"No. I can't ask you in," she said. "My husband was ever so cross when I told him. He'll be home any minute and I shouldn't like him to find you here, especially after you've been across the road."

"But you asked me yesterday . . ."

"I know I did. But that was before I told him. I shouldn't like to tell you what he said. Oh my goodness, this is him coming now."

Carolus turned to face a sour-looking man with grey ginger hair and a well-worn tweed overcoat. He was carrying a despatch case.

"What do you want?" he asked Carolus aggressively.

"A word with you," said Carolus.

"Oh? On what authority?"

"None at all. Your wife was kind enough to say that I might call when you were here."

"She did? Then she had no business to say anything

of the sort. See what it says on the gate? 'No Hawkers, No Circulars'—that means you."

"Thank you," said Carolus. "You left the house shortly before your mother-in-law was killed, I believe? I wonder why you didn't tell the police that."

Pressley's face did not change.

"Are you trying to be funny?" he asked menacingly.

"Now, Harry," said his wife.

"Oh no," said Carolus. "I never try to be funny. I'm in deadly earnest. You *were* out of the house that evening, weren't you?"

"What's it got to do with you?"

"Nothing. But it had a lot to do with Dyke and you didn't tell him. Where did you go?"

"Look here. Clear off, will you? I've never heard such cheek in my life. Asking about my movements. You must be out of your mind."

"But why *didn't* you tell Dyke?" persisted Carolus.

"Because it's no damn business of his what I do, or yours either. Now, if you don't . . ."

"What time were you at the King's Head?"

"Who told you I'd been to the King's Head?"

Carolus thought of the little bird at Mr. Gorringer's ear but said blandly, "Oh things get about, you know. Why don't we talk sensibly about this?"

"Have I got to be questioned by every lay-about that comes to my door?"

"That's for you to decide."

Pressley hesitated then glanced at the windows in the house opposite.

"Come in," he said with no welcoming smile at all.

He hung his coat in the hallway and faced Carolus in the room in which Carolus had been yesterday.

"Now what is it you want? What are you up to?"

"Nothing, really. Just satisfying my curiosity."

"You're not such a bloody fool as to suspect me of these crimes, are you?"

"I haven't got what you could call a suspect yet. But you were out of your home when your mother-in-law was stabbed. And you had had a row with her that evening."

"It's that old bitch opposite again," shouted Pressley. "She put you up to this. I'll charge her with slander very soon. The whole thing's ridiculous, anyway. I went to the pub that night, yes. I often go. So would you if you had a mother-in-law like mine. Trying to tell me how to lead my life. Interfering between my wife and me. No one could stand her."

"What about the man most likely to know her true character? Her husband?"

"Poor old chap. He'd gone under to her long ago. I make no bones about it. Dead or not, I say straight out I couldn't stand her. That's not to say I did her in, as you should know if you've got any sense at all. It'd be too obvious, wouldn't it? Besides, what about the other two? Think I popped over to Crabtree Avenue and did them as well just for the fun of it? Don't be silly."

"All the same, Mr. Pressley, you *didn't* tell the police you were out that night, did you?"

"They never asked me. Why should I tell them anything unless they ask? I don't like them anyway. And my movements can be checked, as you found out when you heard I was in the King's Head."

"See anyone there you knew?" asked Carolus casually.

"One or two from Crabtree Avenue I've seen there before. Man called Turnwright, who can't stand most of the others over there."

"Was the park-keeper there?"

"Old Slatter? No. He uses the Mitre."

"Thanks, Pressley. You've been a good witness, after all."

"Well, don't come round again, that's all, because I've had about enough of it."

Nine

CAROLUS decided to leave for his home in Newminster for a couple of days away from the depressing atmosphere of Albert Park. He wanted to sort things out in his mind before he proceeded to the third murder, the second in order of incidence. The beginnings of a notion were beginning to form in his mind and he wanted to review his facts and see what evidence he had for it.

Perhaps 'facts' was too strong a word for what had guided him to his embryo theory. Perhaps, he admitted wearily as he drove home, he never would have more. It was unlike previous cases in more senses than one. A homicidal maniac broke all precedents.

He slept soundly but was awakened in what seemed to him the small hours by a knock on his bedroom door, not the sharp purposeful knock of Mrs. Stick but a casual-sounding, unfamiliar knock with loose knuckles. He called "Come in!" to be faced with unwelcome entry of his least favourite pupil, Rupert Priggley. This precocious youth with his intolerably sophisticated manner and air of condescension to the adult world had more than once associated himself with Carolus's investigations, for his parents, long since divorced, had a way of leaving him for the holidays at a loose end but amply provided with pocket money.

"What on earth do you mean by disturbing me in the middle of the night?" Carolus demanded.

"It's nearly 8 o'clock," returned Priggley, "and I bring news that will make you leap with boyish excitement."

"Get to hell out of here. Where are your parents?"

"Mummy's on a yacht at Ibiza with a Greek, I understand. As for daddy, the least said the better."

"What do you mean, news?"

"You wouldn't be interested in anything connected with Albert Park, would you, sir? No I thought not. Creeping off there at the end of term without a word to the only human being who has ever been in the least helpful to you in what you so cornily call your investigations."

"You're an impertinent little wretch. Call Mrs. Stick."

"It's all right. I've told her. She's bringing your tea. She was delighted at my news, I can tell you."

Carolus looked about for something to throw.

"What news, you hell-hound?" he shouted.

"It's over. Finished. Wound-up. You've been wasting your time. They've got the Stabber."

"What do you mean?"

"I went over on the motor bike last night. I thought you might need keeping an eye on."

"Don't end sentences with prepositions. Well?"

"Well, the whole place was in a ferment. The Stabber

had been caught. *In flagrante delicto,* I gathered."

"You mean there has been another murder?"

"Really, sir," said Priggley reproachfully. "Your lust for blood in insatiable. No, not another murder. But as near as, dammit. The man was actually arrested concealed in a front garden of Crabtree Avenue with the famous butcher's knife under his coat. What more do you want?"

"Who was it?"

"Total stranger, apparently. No one connected with any of the cases. Man from New Cross. I can't tell you his name yet."

"You wouldn't be trying to pull my leg, would you?"

Priggley sighed elaborately and produced a morning paper with large headlines—ALBERT PARK: MAN TAKEN TO STATION. Carolus began to read "Residents in the district of Albert Park slept more peacefully tonight for . . ." "Quick action by Police Constable Golding . . ." "The man was still at the station at a late hour . . ." No name was mentioned.

"So you see," said Priggley, "this time you've had it. The best I could do to save your face was to put it about that the police were acting on a tip-off from you."

"Idiot."

"Don't get irascible, sir. This was bound to happen sooner or later. You can't be lucky every time."

"Out of my sight," said Carolus.

"I'll wait downstairs. You'll need my warm-hearted sympathy."

But worse things came to Carolus. He had scarcely finished breakfast when Mr. Gorringer was announced.

"Ah, Deene! Ah, Priggley," he said. "I thought you were spending your holiday with the Hollingbournes?"

"I was, sir, but unfortunately one of their children was caught with a glass of port and I was held to blame. I felt it more tactful to withdraw."

"I'll go into that at a more opportune moment. Meanwhile, Deene, I come to congratulate you. A splendid job. Splendid. In so short a time, too. I am referring to the arrest last night."

"Oh that. I had nothing to do with it. And it was not an arrest, as far as I can gather. A man is held for questioning."

Mr. Gorringer gave his dramatic chuckle.

"Come, Deene, you are too modest. You won't convince me that it was not on your information that the police acted in so timely a fashion. It bears all the marks of your peculiar talent. I said to Mrs. Gorringer this morning, 'another triumph for Deene' and she replied wittily, though somewhat obscurely 'Albert Park and the lion.'"

"I've only just heard of this development," said Carolus.

"Now, Deene. You can't catch old birds with chaff, you know. It is true I have asked you, for the sake of the school's fair name, not to associate yourself publicly with these matters, but here you are amongst . . ." he glanced at Priggley, "you are in the presence of your headmaster. You must tell me how you achieved this prompt and welcome result."

"I'm not sure there is a result. If there is I had nothing to do with it and it goes flat against any possible ideas I was forming." Carolus seemed to forget his audience. "How can it have been a stranger to the district?" he asked. "How can a man who has till now shown such cunning—even if a madman's cunning—have walked straight into a police trap? Not even a trap. He must have known Crabtree Avenue was being watched."

Mr. Gorringer rose dramatically, his large ears flushed crimson.

"You are not going to suggest, I trust, that the arrested man is *not* the murderer?"

"I don't know. I haven't enough to go on to suggest anything. But I don't see how it can be."

"He was, I suppose," began Mr. Gorringer with lofty scorn, "a peaceful citizen enjoying the evening air. He just happened to have with him a lethal weapon similar to, or identical with, that used in three recent murders in the same area."

"Stranger things have happened." said Carolus.

"You tempt me to speak incivilly, Deene. What you suggest is beyond all credibility."

"The truth so often is. I must get over to Albert Park."

"You are not proposing to return to that suburb?"

"At once, yes. Whatever this is, it provides a god-sent opportunity of clearing up one or two small points."

Mr. Gorringer prepared to leave.

"You confound all logical expectations, Deene. You intend once again to pit your theories against the wisdom of an experienced police force and against all factual probability. I despair of appealing to your reason."

He left the room without taking his leave.

"It does seem a bit off, you know, sir. This character they've arrested must have been on the job."

"So far as we know he has not been charged yet. He was taken to a police station and according to this paper was 'still there at a late hour' last night. Dyke is no fool."

Whatever Carolus, or the headmaster, or the Press, thought about the incident of the previous evening, the people of Albert Park seemed to have no doubt that their troubles were over. To get rid of Priggley for a time Carolus told him to move about the suburb and later give him a report of public reactions to the news and he presented lively details of conversations overheard in shops, cafés and the Mitre.

"So they've got him!"

"Good job, too!"

"It was about time, that's what I think."

"He was just going to do it again, wasn't he?"

"Still, its a blessing we shall be able to walk about."

And so on.

But Carolus meanwhile was busy. His first call was on Eamon Starkey at his flat on Blackheath. He found the actor finishing a late breakfast.

"I must say I'm relieved," said Starkey.

"Why 'relieved'?"

"Obvious, isn't it? Anyone could be suspected."

Carolus looked at him fixedly.

"Now that it's all over," he said. "Would you like to clear up something that has puzzled me? You made a great point of your alibi for that night. Why did you think it was necessary?"

"Because I hadn't got an alibi, really."

"You were at the Crucible Theatre."

"I went there, yes."

"You mean?"

"Look here, Deene. I saw the other night that you weren't quite satisfied with what I told you. I trust you, for some reason, and would have told you the truth then but for the fact that no one knew who had killed my sister. You must remember that at first there was no reason to think it was one of a series of murders. The police asked me the most searching questions and I naturally used my alibi. They seemed satisfied with it, but you weren't. Were you?"

"No. It occurred to me at once that anyone could wear a mask and shout 'Live, live, live, live' and so on. It would not have to be you."

"It wasn't, on that night. This is what has worried me, till now. A friend of mine, or I thought he was a friend of mine, took it on and no one suspected. Actually all I wanted was to go out for a drink. I didn't go to the Wheatsheaf, of course, but to another pub called the Crown. I got talking there and stayed far too long."

"Did you go on your motor-bike?"

"Good Lord, no! Everyone would have heard me starting it up."

"Unless you wheeled it down the road a little way."

"Well, I didn't, anyway." Starkey stared as though he had suddenly realized something. "You mean I *could* have gone to Albert Park?"

"I don't know. I haven't gone into times and so on. But it had occurred to me."

"Thank God the thing's all cleared up, then."

"A lot of people are saying that. Now I must rush away. See you again, perhaps."

"I hope so," said Starkey genially. "What about coming to see our new show at the Crucible?"

"I'm relieved to hear you calling it a show."

Starkey smiled.

"It's a revival. The most successful thing we've done. It was written by Thomas Wilkinson."

"Neoteric, I understand?"

"Enormously. Will you come?"

"Yes. When all this is cleared up. If your play's still on."

"Is that a promise?"

"It is."

Carolus drove from Blackheath back to Albert Park. He heard from Priggley some more hearsay details of last night's incident, including the fact that young Gates had been present at the time and according to some reports had actually assisted in the arrest. As it was a Saturday afternoon he hoped that Gates might be at home and drove to number 52 Crabtree Avenue.

Stanley Gates came to the door himself, a rather self-satisfied young man with a crewcut, heavy spectacles and a neat moustache. He had a jocular 'old boy' manner which grated somewhat, but he was ready enough to talk of last night's incidents, indeed had done so to a number of reporters.

"Most extraordinary thing I ever saw," he began chirpily when he had asked Carolus to sit down. "I still can hardly believe it happened. I decided to give the avenue the once-over before joining the old folks in the other room for their television session. They don't seem to enjoy it if I'm not there, being bored stiff, of course. I went out . . ."

"What time would that have been?"

"I was forgetting that. You sleuths are all for the unforgiving minute, aren't you? Must have been just after seven. It was a fairly bright night. I thought I'd just walk up to the top and back, and see if anything was doing. Vigilante stuff."

Carolus had the feeling that the story had been told several times before and had grown more detailed with repetition.

"I passed one or two bods in the lower part of the

avenue. Old Goggins walking home. Mrs. Sparkett. I passed a copper who came out of Perth Avenue and went on down Crabtree."

"Did you know him?"

"By sight. Yes. He's one of our regulars since this happened. The police have done what they can, you know. I knew he'd be hanging about for the next hour or so. Oh, by the way, I looked in the garden of the empty house where the first body was found. Number 46. Nothing in sight. I passed the park gates opposite Perth Avenue and as I reached the upper part of the avenue I saw this figure."

"Which figure?" asked Carolus annoyingly.

"This figure of the man we ran in. The Stabber in fact, though you wouldn't have thought it. It seemed he had been waiting in one of the gardens because he seemed suddenly to materialize in front of me."

"Which garden?"

"Well, it might have been Turnwright's. Somewhere about there. Turnwright's is 28."

"What did you notice about this man?"

"His most extraordinary behaviour. He was capering, old man, I can only call it capering, up the pavement in front of me. The next thing I saw was that he was wearing a raincoat."

"Did it fit him?"

"What d'you mean? Of course it fitted him. Why shouldn't it?"

"Never mind. Do go on."

"He was wearing a raincoat, a cloth cap and glasses. So I thought to myself, this is it. Well, there couldn't be much doubt of it, could there?"

"Yes," said Carolus. "What did you do next?"

"What would you have done? Gone up and asked

him if he was the Stabber? No, I went and found this policeman I had seen. Golding, his name is. I told him exactly what I had seen and no more. He had the sense to realize this was It and we walked back up the avenue to where I'd seen him last."

"And of course he'd disappeared."

"Yes. But we soon found him. Most extraordinary thing. He was in one of the gardens making a sort of squeaking noise. Like a mouse."

"Have you ever heard a mouse?"

"I suppose not. But this is the sort of noise they'd make. The creature was barking mad. Well, we've always thought so, haven't we? Barking. We walked up to him and he began to threaten us with this dam' great knife."

"To *threaten* you?"

"Yes, old man. I thought this was It. I started . . ."

"How do you mean, 'threaten' you?"

"Just that. He threatened us."

"Are you sure he wasn't merely showing you the knife?"

"I ask you. What would he want to show it for if he wasn't threatening?"

"What did he want to squeak for if it wasn't to call your attention?"

"I tell you. He was batty."

"Exactly. But go on. You and the policeman disarmed him."

"Well, yes. It wasn't so easy . . ."

"Did he say anything?"

"He was babbling. He'd done them all, he said. With that same knife we'd taken off him. His name was Samuel Hoskins and he lived in New Cross. He'd intended to do another one tonight and he did not know how many more. You should have seen his eyes! He had the most beastly stare I've ever seen. Talk about homicidal mania."

"How did the policeman manage?"

"Old Goggins came up just then and we got him to phone for a squad car. But we had to wait with him there for about ten minutes and it wasn't pleasant, I can tell you."

"Big man?"

"Medium size. Pretty powerful customer, though. They say lunatics are unnaturally strong. I can quite believe it."

"Did he struggle?"

"Not after we'd got the butcher's knife off him. I don't know what happened later. I wanted to go along with them to the Station but the copper in charge thanked me and said it wouldn't be necessary."

"I thank you, too, Mr. Gates. Seen Viola Whitehill lately?"

"Viola? Yes. I see her. But she's not really my type. Why do you ask?"

"Curiosity," said Carolus. "It's a vice of mine."

He was not surprised to find, when he reached Inverness Road and bought a newspaper, that Samuel Hoskins had left the police station without being charged. The police, it seemed, had satisfied themselves that he could not have been responsible for any of the murders. His family had undertaken to look after him 'for', one of them said, 'we've had this sort of trouble before with Uncle. He's perfectly well-behaved generally and the doctors say there's no cause for anxiety but we shall have to see that nothing of this sort occurs again.'

"Now, I suppose," said Priggley that evening, "you're

going to congratulate yourself on being so remarkably shrewd."

Carolus smiled.

"It didn't need much shrewdness," he said. "But it served one good purpose."

"He was one of these confession fiends, I suppose?"

"Yes. There are always a few after much-publicized murders. They're a nuisance to the police. Dyke had to check up on the man but I don't suppose he was fooled for a moment."

"And now?"

"Now Joyce Ribbing," said Carolus shortly.

Ten

CAROLUS thought that six o'clock in the evening would be a good time to call on Goggins and his wife. His ring was answered by Goggins himself who stared at him suspiciously. Carolus explained himself, wisely adding something to suggest that Goggins as a Vigilante and an observant man might have sources of information untapped by the police.

When he was first shown into the sitting-room, Carolus thought he had disturbed the couple at tea, for the pot was still standing there.

"Stone cold, I'm afraid," said Ada Goggins. "We have tea at four. But have a cake."

Carolus refused but Ada bit off more than half a cream bun and continued to munch happily. Carolus discovered that one meal in this house only really ended when another began, at least for the hostess. Goggins was smoking, appropriately, a meerschaum pipe.

"I don't know whether there's anything I can tell you," he said ponderously.

"He was alone that evening," said Ada Goggins, attacking an eclair.

"Which evening?" Carolus asked.

"The evening when Joyce was murdered. That's what you want to see us about, isn't it?"

"Partly, yes. But the first murder . . ."

"We don't know anything about that. Never seen the woman, to my knowledge."

"You had a friend here that evening, I believe?"

"Did we? Oh yes. Williamson from my husband's office," said Ada, scattering cake crumbs from her mouth as she remembered the occasion.

"I am what you might call semi-retired," explained Goggins. "Williamson is an accountant in my firm, Marryat, Goggins, Richmond and Partners. We're chartered accountants. Offices in Chancery Lane."

"He doesn't want to know all that, you old silly," put in Ada, returning to the bread and butter. "It's the murders he's interested in."

"What time did Mr. Williamson arrive that evening?"

"About this time, I should say," replied Goggins thoughtfully.

"And stayed till?"

"Nine-ish, wasn't it, dear?" said Ada.

"About nine," replied Goggins judiciously. "Scarcely surprising that we heard nothing, therefore."

"There's not much traffic in Crabtree Avenue at night?"

"Very little indeed."

"Have you yourselves got a car?"

"No. We had until two years ago but we've given it up."

"You're not pestered by young people on motor-bikes?"

"Oh no. It's a quiet residential neighbourhood," said Goggins seriously, "that is why we selected it."

"But you must sometimes hear a motor-bike?"

"Occasionally, I dare say. Very occasionally."

"You don't remember hearing one that night—when your friend Mr. Williamson was here?"

They both looked thoughtful.

"I have no recollection of it," said Goggins.

"I do seem to remember one about that time," Ada said brightly. "Several evenings about then, I think. I can't be sure it was that night, though. Why? Had the Stabber a motor-bike?"

She had turned away from the tea-things and opened a large box of chocolates.

"You never noticed any strangers about the avenue, I suppose? I mean before any of this happened."

"Tell him about the tall woman," said Ada, unwrapping a chocolate.

"Oh that. I scarcely think that would be of interest," replied Goggins. "But I'll tell you, for what it's worth. It was about ten days or a fortnight before the unfortunate schoolmistress was found. I was returning to the house late one afternoon at about five o'clock in fact..."

"Oh get *on!*" pleaded his wife, battling with a hard centre.

"I was about to open the gate when I noticed a somewhat tall woman coming down the steps from the front door. Presuming it was a friend or acquaintance of my wife who had just emerged, I raised my hat and opened the gate for her, at the same time saying good-evening."

"Trying to get off," said Ada gaily, playing for safety with a peppermint cream.

"Did she reply?" asked Carolus.

"She bowed, and passed on. There was something odd about her."

"Hold it!" said Carolus with uncharacteristic excitement. "That very expression was used of another person observed in this case. Please try to answer this, Mr. Goggins. *What* was odd about her?"

"It's very hard to say. When I came in I mentioned the occurrence to my wife and she told me that no one had called, no one had rung the bell, no one had been seen by her for the last hour."

"You mean that it was odd she should be coming out of your gate? But you *said* there was something odd about *her*."

"There was," said Goggins obstinately. "There was. I noticed it at the time. But I cannot for the life of me tell you what it was."

"Was she preternaturally tall?"

"She was tall, but it was not that. I don't notice women's clothes much, but I gained the impression that she was somewhat overdressed. Yet I don't think it was that."

"You had never seen her before?"

"No. Yet I had a strange, almost psychic sense of recognition."

"Did you see her again?"

"Never. It was as though I had seen a ghost."

"When you say 'recognition'—who did she remind you of?"

"No one, at the time. But later it occurred to me when I was travelling up to town with a neighbour of ours named Heatherwell that if he had a sister she might well have resembled the woman I saw."

"Did you mention that to Heatherwell?"

"I did just ask him if he had a sister, and he seemed

almost to resent the enquiry. 'No, certainly not', he said, and I refrained from telling him why I asked."

Ada's face was contorted by the mastication of an obstinately cohesive caramel.

"Could the Stabber be a woman?" she asked.

"I see no absolute and final reason against it," said Carolus. "May we move forward, now, to the night of the second murder?"

"That we can tell you more about," said Ada who had mastered her difficulties and was seeking more with a burnt almond. "I played Bridge with poor Joyce that very evening and Lionel," Carolus remembered that Goggins was Lionel, "discovered the body in the morning. We knew nothing about the lover, though."

"My dear, I hardly think . . ."

"Well, he was her lover, wasn't he?"

"You were playing Bridge at Mrs. Whitehill's?"

"Yes. We started after tea. About half-past four. It was nearly nine when Joyce said she *had* to go. I stayed on to supper."

"Nothing unusual occurred during that time?"

"A few sharp words from Stella Whitehill to her niece. Joyce and I won twenty-seven shillings."

"And Joyce Ribbing went off quite cheerfully?"

"Quite. Said something about neglecting her old man and fled. Nobody thought anything of it at the time. There had only been one murder, you see. She wasn't the sort of woman you'd think anything could happen to. Capable, you know, and downright."

"What time did you come home?"

"About ten. I had left Lionel some food. He doesn't eat much, anyway."

"So you must have passed within a couple of yards of the body as you walked up to your front door?"

"Must have, mustn't I? Nothing in that, though. We don't have an outside light and the body had been shoved right under the front hedge."

"Still, if you'd turned that way you'd have seen it."

"*If* I'd turned that way. But fortunately I didn't. I should have had a fit."

"What I'm getting at," said Carolus patiently, "is that when the murderer left the body there he did not very much care whether it was discovered before morning or not. He could see the lights in your hall. If it was someone who knew all about your movements he knew that you would be coming home from Whitehill's and might easily see it. If he knew nothing, he still must have thought you might have to let the dog out, or receive late callers, or something. He did not mind how soon the body was discovered so long as he was out of the immediate vicinity. He made no attempt to conceal it, did he?"

"None, beyond putting it well under the hedge."

"Where you, Mr. Goggins, first saw it in the morning?"

"Yes. I looked out to see what kind of day it was and saw it at once."

"We were just having a cup of tea and a biscuit," put in Ada. "It quite upset Lionel. He has a very sensitive stomach. Well, its not very nice to find someone you know lying murdered in your garden, is it?"

"I've never had the experience," admitted Carolus, "but I should think it was highly unpleasant. So the assumption is that Joyce Ribbing was murdered almost outside your gate."

"That is so," said Goggins.

"And you were in the house the whole time?"

"I was."

"Television?"

"Yes, indeed. My wife, Mr. Deene, is what I believe is termed a Bridge fiend, and I have become accustomed to passing the hours of her absence with one or another of the programmes."

"I see. So even if there had been quite a disturbance in the street you might not have heard it?"

"I certainly shouldn't. The set is in the back room."

"And your next-door neighbours?"

"We have no acquaintance with them but I have observed that both have aerials. Well, it would be strange if they hadn't, wouldn't it?"

"It would indeed. Yet it still seems to me even stranger that a woman can be murdered a few yards from a number of dwelling-houses at nine o'clock on a winter evening in England and no one be the wiser."

"One of the blessings of television," said Ada Goggins gaily as she wiped the chocolate from her fingers.

"There must have been some sound," Carolus pointed out.

"The police are of the opinion that there was almost none, I understand. The stabbing was an expert job," remarked Goggins.

"Even so . . ."

"And what about the first one?" asked Ada. "Up the road, I mean. No one heard that."

"True."

"We, in this avenue," said Goggins laboriously, "are of the opinion that the Stabber is someone known by sight in the district. That would account for the absence of alarm in the victims. They had no cause to scream."

"I see your point," said Carolus watching him narrowly. "But what about Viola Whitehill? She certainly did not know the man she saw in the car."

"She has told my wife that she tried to scream, but could not. The sound simply would not come."

"That might have been the case with the others," Carolus pointed out.

"All three?" said Goggins. "It seems unlikely."

"You knew Joyce Ribbing well?"

"Pretty well," said Ada, at last putting the used tea-things and the empty chocolate box on the tray. "She was devoted to her children," she added unexpectedly. "One of those possessive mothers who insist on doing everything with the younger generation."

"Really?"

"Yes. Inclined to boast about it, too. She once told me she had all Roddy's confidence. That's the son—a boy of sixteen. At Uppingham, I believe. Or is it Radley?"

"A mother who believes she has all the confidence of a sixteen-year-old son is asking for disillusionment," observed Carolus tritely.

"Joyce would insist on it. She was one of those rather straining women who keep young with their children, use their slang, beat them at games and have long confidential talks with them," said Ada rather unkindly. "That's what made it all the more unexpected about this man in Chelsea."

"I wonder how that came to be known in Albert Park," said Carolus.

"Oh, everything's known here. I think it first came through the Tuckmans. I'm not sure. Anyway, the Doctor knew."

"So I gather."

"Though he may not have known how far it had gone."

"And how far had it gone?"

Goggins coughed and Ada shrugged her shoulders.

"Though I don't believe she planned to go off with the man," she said after that eloquent lacuna. "She was too wrapped up in the children for that."

"Did you know Turrell?"

"Was that his name? No. We only knew there was someone with a flat in Chelsea. Anything else you want to know? Because I'm starving. Why don't you stay and take pot luck with us? Lionel scarcely touches anything and I don't like eating alone. It's all cold. I'll have it ready in a minute."

Carolus excused himself on the grounds that he wanted urgently to see Mrs. Whitehill.

"Good time to catch her," said Ada. "She doesn't eat till some unearthly hour. That night when Joyce . . . when we were playing Bridge, it was past nine. I don't know how she holds out."

When Carolus was outside he hesitated, then set off briskly uphill. But like an embodiment of his recent thoughts during the conversation of Goggins a figure appeared on the pavement ahead of him, a tall woman walking mincingly away.

There was certainly something odd about this apparition, but unlike Goggins, Carolus knew exactly what it was. Even before he saw the face he knew why Goggins had thought her overdressed and so on. He decided to count on the luck which rarely deserted him in small crises of this kind and as he drew level with the tall woman looked her squarely in the face and said "Good evening, Mr. Heatherwell."

The tall woman stopped and gasped.

"How *dare* you?" she said in a high cracking voice.

"Am I making a mistake?" said Carolus.

"You . . . you . . . Please go away," cried the tall woman. "You've no right to speak to me."

"I only said good evening," Carolus pointed out, looking at her large hands and feet. "You *are* Heatherwell, aren't you?"

"My name's Nora," said the tall woman.

"Tonight, yes. But normally it's Heatherwell."

"Leave me alone!"

"I want a little talk with you."

Suddenly, to the complete surprise of Carolus, he received a fierce jab on the chin, delivered with a large clenched fist, a jab which knocked him back against the railings.

"Now will you clear off?" said the tall woman in a voice which had suddenly dropped to bass.

"I must say that as Nora you've got a pretty good punch. But I shall be ready for the next one. I wish you'd be sensible and answer a few questions. How long have you been doing this?"

There was a silence in which Carolus felt that sanity was asserting itself.

"A couple of months or more," said Heatherwell at last, unhappily.

"An irresistible impulse. Does your wife know?"

"Yes. She's worried to death, of course. She went away as soon as . . . it started."

"Did it start before the first murder?"

This seemed to trouble Heatherwell.

"Yes. It did," he said. "But it was nothing then. Very rare, I mean. I first did it as a boy. I thought it was a joke then. It hasn't been that lately."

"Do you remember whether this happened on the night of the first murder?"

"Well, yes, it did. You can imagine how I felt next

morning. I must have passed the woman's body. After that I seemed quite unable to withstand the impulse and went out almost every night."

"So you were out on the nights of the other two murders?"

"I must have been, yes."

"Did anyone recognize you?"

"Not to my knowledge. I can never be sure of that. No one said anything. *You're* not going to talk about it, are you?"

"I can't promise that. You see I'm trying to investigate these murders."

"What's that got to do with it?"

"I don't know. Perhaps nothing. If that's so you've chosen a very unlucky time for these excursions of yours. Do you go far from here?"

"Only just round the park."

"You don't drive about like that?"

"No. I haven't a car. Besides there would be no point in that."

"Why not?"

"You see, its the danger . . ."

"Yes. I know something about transvestism. And here there was a particular danger, wasn't there? From the Stabber, I mean."

Heatherwell hesitated and said—"Yes." The grotesque make-up concealed any expression there might be on his face.

"Was it the murder, the idea of a man looking for a lonely woman, which caused you to carry on this, do you think?"

"I don't know. I suppose so because soon after that first murder it became as I told you an almost nightly occurrence. I wanted to see what would happen."

"What did you think would happen?"

"I didn't know. I knew there was danger. From the murderer, from the police, from recognition. It was that which drew me, I think."

"How did you come to be in the Goggins' front garden one day?"

"It was a mad idea. I had been walking round for some time and no one took any notice. I went into the park and even talked to Slatter, the park-keeper whom I knew, without being recognized."

"Sure?"

"Pretty sure. Slatter would have said something. On my way home that day I thought I would call on Ada Goggins and see whether she knew who I was. Just as I was going to ring the bell I saw Goggins coming up the road and decided to flee. I was only just in time. He held the gate open for me, but must have noticed something because some days later he kept staring at me and asked if I had a sister. I suppose that is how you came to know who I was."

"Yes. Now I've got to warn you, Heatherwell. You say you want danger . . ."

"Not now. At this minute I'm simply humiliated and disgusted and can't think how I can ever have indulged in such lunacy."

"Yes. But in certain moods you look for danger of a peculiar kind. I've got to tell you that if I have any understanding at all of this case you are *in* danger, all the time. Danger of a very serious, in fact a mortal kind. I am not going further into details. But I warn you."

"You mean, danger of prosecution?"

"For transvestism? It is far more serious than that. Far more. Has your wife returned to you yet?"

"No. As a matter of fact I don't know whether she'll return to me."

"You're alone in the house, then?"

"Yes."

"Don't ask anyone in. Even if it is someone you think you know. Don't be alone with anyone, if you can help it. And don't, on any account, admit to anyone what you have been doing."

"That's scarcely likely, is it?"

"Your wife knows already. Does anyone else?"

"I don't think so. But I can't be sure. Goggins seems to have half guessed."

"For heaven's sake don't let them."

"You seem very concerned for me. I don't know who you are."

"My name's Deene. It's not only for you I'm concerned, Heatherwell. I want to prevent another murder."

"You mean, you suspect me?"

"I suspect everyone till I find out who was responsible. But it's not only that. I have a particular reason for telling you to be extremely careful."

"You mean, the Stabber? One thing I realized was that there wasn't much danger for me. All the women killed were short. It would take a giant to kill me with that particular downward blow."

"For God's sake, pull yourself together, Heatherwell, and don't talk like that. You simply have no conception of this case. I've said as much as I possibly can and if you ignore what I've told you, you're mad."

"Perhaps I am a little mad. I must be to do this, mustn't I?"

"I'm not an alienist. I don't know. But I know your life's in danger. Is this your house?"

"No. Number 32."

"Then go home at once and don't let anyone in. You're working in the daytime?"

"Yes."

"All right. Good night."

He watched the grotesque figure till it had disappeared into number 32.

Eleven

NEXT morning Carolus surprised Priggley by telling him quite seriously that he must leave Albert Park and not return to it.

"This is no longer a nice cosy case in which I can allow you to play around," he said. "I'm convinced now that there's very real danger here and not merely for lonely women going home at night. I'm not going into it all, but you've got to go."

Priggley protested.

"Don't start getting earnest, sir. It doesn't suit you. There's no more danger, as you call it, than in any other of your how-d'ye-do's. Just because three women . . ."

"No, Priggley, this is final. I may be wrong about this case. The man who killed those women may be miles away or dead, but I'm not going to take the responsibility. You must go back to Newminster."

"*Not* to Hollingbourne's, sir? I really can't take another round of teenagers' parties."

"Away from here you're no responsibility of mine, thank God."

"All right. All right. I'll go like a lamb. But on one condition. You'll let me in for the kill, as it were. The final exposition, which you seem to consider your forte."

"If there is one, and if by then I'm satisfied that there's no further danger."

"How you harp on that word."

"I want your promise that you won't come back here unless I send for you."

"Promises now. How square can you get? All right. Cross my heart. Are you really on to something, though, sir?"

"I think so."

"Well, you seem pretty leisurely about it. How do you know there won't be another murder while you're making your enquiries?"

"I don't," said Carolus grimly. "That is exactly what worries me."

"I don't suppose the police are actually hilarious about it. You'd better take your finger out, sir. If it's *that* full of 'danger'."

"Out," said Carolus. "On to that motor-cycle of yours and away."

" 'I go, I go; look how I go, Swifter than arrow from the Tartar's bow'."

"M.N.D. again last term?" said Carolus, and was relieved to see Priggley disappear.

He was faced again with the dilemma which troubled him in most of his cases—was he justified in going his solitary way, making his exhaustive personal enquiries, sometimes doing no more than absorb the atmosphere of a crime, while the murderer was still at large and liable to strike again? It seemed pedantic, almost heartless. Yet what else could he do? He was no policeman with the forces of order at his command. He was no

Holmes, who would arm himself with a stout cudgel or even a pistol on occasion and go flying, as it were, at the throat of the enemy. He was—outwardly at least—a mild history master whose private passion was the investigation of crime by his own methods, in his own time, through what talents of perspicacity he possessed. He could not change his character or procedure because he believed that another blow might fall before he had reached any useful conclusion. He could only peg away, question after question, encouraging confidences, noting demeanour, drawing makeshift conclusions, until the big conclusion was drawn. Sometimes, as in his advice to Heatherwell, he might do something to check one dangerous possibility. But on the whole his part was rarely an active one and he did not aspire to those feats of agility, heroism, and unarmed combat which made the exploits of his rivals, particularly in America, so exciting.

Back to the grindstone, he thought at last, and set out to see Joyce Ribbing's sister in Sevenoaks.

Beryl, more frequently and considerately known as Bee, was a hardy, dog-owning, golf-playing woman, married to a company director named Knapstick. Carolus found her at home in a breezy little house surrounded with flourishing spring bulbs, an MG car at her gate and a poodle in the hall.

"About Joyce?" she said loudly. "All right. I suppose so. Come in. They haven't caught the creature, have they?"

"Not so far as I know," said Carolus. "But I'm not the police. Just a private individual deeply interested."

"Fair enough," said Bee. "Have a drink? Good. I feel like a snifter at this time of day. What kind of madman was it who killed my sister?"

"A very clever madman. Three murders in one area within a few weeks and no arrest as yet argues considerable intelligence."

"Or luck," said Bee. "More soda? Yes, it could be luck, couldn't it? Jack the Ripper did two in one night. Cigarette?"

"Jack the Ripper's murders were in 1888 and 1889 when the police force had very little knowledge of forensic psychology."

"How many were there?" asked Bee.

"Nine occasions. Ten women. But they were all prostitutes. And all in the East End."

"I daresay. But how do you know there won't be ten of these? The only difference I see is that the district *and* the victims are more respectable."

"The original Ripper was never identified," reflected Carolus. "There have been some interesting theories about that, but nothing very convincing."

"You think this one will be caught?"

"I hope so. I hope very soon, before . . ."

"Exactly," said Bee. "Before there's another. But how? How can one of these mass murderers be caught unless in the act?"

"I don't know," said Carolus. "But tell me about your sister."

"Joyce? Very much a mother. Devoted to the kids. But seemed afraid she was missing something. The doctor's a bit of a stick. Conscientious and sound but not exactly sparkling. Poor old Joyce wanted a break now and again. Sometimes she would come over here. Seemed to think we knew how to live. Well, we try."

"You've said a great deal, Mrs. Knapstick. You and she were great friends?"

"I shouldn't say that, really. Oh, I know the line—

'there is no friend like a sister' and that. But I don't think we were so intimate. It was months before she told me about her young man."

"But she did tell you?"

"Eventually, yes. And pretty ghastly he sounded."

"You never met him?"

"No. I doubt if he ever came down to this part of the world. One of these metropolitan types who never go anywhere out of the sound of Bow bells except to Cannes for a month."

"Wealthy?"

"That I don't know. Joyce never discussed it. She and I both have a little money of our own but can't touch the capital. Its not much use nowadays—about five hundred a year each."

"Will that go to Dr. Ribbing now?"

"No. The will was made before either of us were married. Hers will come to me. Hardly an inducement for murder, though. Have another drink?"

"May I ask something that will seem rather impertinent?"

"Go ahead."

"Was this man Turrell the first . . . I mean since your sister's marriage?"

"I should say undoubtedly. For one thing I would have known. For another she wasn't at all the type for these fashionable infidelities. I think she was carried off her feet by Turrell. He was completely out of character."

"When did it start?"

"Some time last winter. A bit more than a year ago."

"And was either of them . . . getting tired of it?"

"I don't think so. It had become rather prosaic, I gathered. Joyce never dreamt of breaking up her marriage for it and Turrell—well, you can imagine

Turrell's attitude when I tell you that they met once a week as regularly as clockwork."

"Yes. I see."

"There was absolutely nothing of a *grande passion* about it, if that's what you think. When I say Joyce was carried off her feet at first, I mean by the whole thing. She'd become stale, down in that dreary suburb, and this meant quite simply, a nice change."

"Yet Dr. Ribbing knew?"

"Joyce thought so, but they never discussed it."

"She wasn't quite as frank as you are, perhaps?"

"Am I frank? I think I just take a very ordinary view of things. I should have thought Joyce was rather frank, but it needs more than frankness to tell your husband you're having an affair for the first time since you married him. Especially with two children. You haven't met the doctor yet?"

"No. I haven't met Turrell, either. I intend to, of course."

"You don't *suspect* them, do you? That would be too absurd."

"Suspect. Suspect. I don't know what to make of the word in this case. I don't think that even Jack the Ripper's victims were chosen *quite* by chance. Christie's certainly weren't. Nor were Heath's."

"You mean you suspect that this Stabber character had something to do with Joyce?"

"Something to do with Albert Park, anyway."

"That's pretty obvious, isn't it. But if you're thinking in terms of motive Joyce is out. Who in the world had any reason to kill her?"

"Yet someone did kill her. Person or Persons Unknown."

"I don't dispute that. Though you sleuths look so

much *round* everything that had death come in any other way I honestly believe you'd have talked of the chances of suicide. Or a wave of suicides. One for the road?"

Carolus came away from Bee Knapstick's cheerful home with a new resolution. He would stick to his line of enquiry but intensify it by moving right into the pious gloom of Albert Park. If it could be arranged—and he thought he saw a way—he would stay in Crabtree Avenue itself and wake and pass his days among the villas and avenues and basements and railings and television sets of that forbiddingly respectable suburb. Though he did not want to admit it, he was reduced now to hoping for a piece of luck, something to occur which might give him a firmer lead than the vaporous theory with which he had been playing.

It was not to facilitate his enquiries. He could make those while still sleeping at night in his comfortable home in Newminster. It was to try to see the place as its people saw it, to take his evening wallop in the doubtless exclusive saloon bar of the Mitre, to hear and see and perhaps sense what was going on.

Somewhere here, just out of reach, perhaps, was that elusive thing he was not ashamed to call a clue. Something, sooner or later, must break. Dyke, no doubt, had people doing what he was about to do, drinking it all in. For him, Carolus, there was no other way. However distasteful it might be he would become a temporary resident of Albert Park.

Besides, he had not merely been frightening poor Heatherwell last night in an attempt to discourage his unfortunate mania. There really was danger for that man and perhaps for others and Carolus could do something to lessen that danger.

He rang the bell of number 32.

A lean weak-faced man opened the door, easily recognizable as 'the tall woman' in normal clothes.

"Oh it's you," he said, seeming relieved rather than ashamed or reproachful. "Come in."

"Look here, Heatherwell. I want to make a suggestion. Your wife's away indefinitely, you say, and you're quite alone. Would it be possible for me to be your paying guest for a week or two?"

The man's startled weak eyes watched him closely.

"I really meant what I said last night," went on Carolus. "You are in danger, in more ways than one. I think it would be safer for you, and perhaps others, if I stayed with you."

"To spy on me," Heatherwell said, almost in a whisper.

"No. But, if you like, to spy on the whole district. I'm not moving fast enough. I'm getting worried and want to be on the spot."

"There's no one to look after this house," said Heatherwell. "Not even a char. I do what I can but I'm in town all day."

"It certainly doesn't look neglected. And there being no one here suits me excellently. I don't want it known that I'm here."

A faint smile came to Heatherwell's face.

"You've got some hopes. It would be known at once."

"I don't think so. I'm gambling on that. Eventually, but not at once, if both of us are cautious. You, at any-rate, could be relied on not to say anything?"

"I could, I suppose, so long as I'm . . . all right. But you'd better face it, Deene, I'm a case for a psychiatrist, as you saw last night."

"I'll chance that, too. At least you would not advertize the fact that I'm staying with you."

Heatherwell looked up furtively.

"I haven't agreed yet," he said. "And what could advertize it more than that bloody great car of yours?"

"Oh don't be silly. I shall leave that in a garage. It isn't outside now."

Heatherwell was still thoughtful. Then he made an effort to speak bluntly.

"Look here," he said, "do you suspect me of these murders?"

"I suspect no one person at present," said Carolus steadily.

"But you think I may have done them?"

"You or one of several hundred people."

"I can prove . . ."

"You don't need to. Will you agree to my proposal?"

"I suppose so. I've been too much alone, anyway, since my wife left. There's quite a decent spare bedroom. It hasn't been used for a long time but I could soon get it straight. Only . . ."

"Well?"

"Will you mind if I talk to you? There's a lot I want to get off my mind."

Carolus reflected on the irony of this. So often, in investigations, he had longed to hear those very words and never, till now when it probably would serve no purpose, had he heard them.

"Certainly. Talk as much as you like. Haven't you any friends in the neighbourhood?"

"Friends? No. I've a few acquaintances in this avenue, I suppose. I haven't had a friend for years."

"You mustn't mistake me for one," said Carolus warningly. "I'm an investigator of a kind and can't afford to have friends connected with a case. I'll listen. If I can be of any help I will. But don't count on my confidence if something you tell me *has* to be repeated."

"Oh, I don't think that. It's not about these ghastly murders. It's about my own state of mind. You see . . ."

Carolus settled down with resignation to listen. And Heatherwell was right. Carolus heard nothing that evening that was of any use to him in establishing the identity of the Stabber.

It was eleven o'clock when he went to a clean and pleasant room at the back of the house. Before undressing, however, he did a most uncharacteristic thing—he locked the door.

He had been asleep some time when he was curtly awakened, not by anything in the house but by a series of sounds in Crabtree Avenue. He thought afterwards that he must have had Priggley on his unconscious mind to be so sensitive to these particular noises, for they were of someone starting a motor-bike nearby and riding away.

Who, he wondered sleepily, who connected with the case had motor-bikes? Before returning to sleep he could remember only the motor-scooters of Grace Buller and Eamon Starkey. Unfortunately, from where he was at the back of the house the sounds, though sufficient to wake a light sleeper like Carolus, were too confused for him to distinguish between engines.

Twelve

VIOLA WHITEHILL opened the door.

"Oh yes," she said without enthusiasm when Carolus had explained himself. "We heard you were coming. You've been round to Goggins, haven't you? I suppose you want to hear about that ghastly experience of mine."

She looked and sounded sulky, not less so when Carolus said shortly—"It's your aunt I wanted to see."

"Well, you'd better come in then; she's in the drawing-room."

Stella Whitehill, rather heavily dressed, was playing Patience in a room that looked like a setting for a Victorian melodrama. Carolus would have liked—out of sheer human curiosity—to have made his first question one about this and expected to hear that the house with everything in it had been inherited from grandparents and unchanged.

He ventured to say that it was a charming period room.

"I don't know about period," said Stella. "It has

been in the Whitehill family since it was built. My husband's grandfather, Dr. Frederick Whitehill, was its first tenant."

"Indeed? That's interesting," said Carolus. And it was. That anyone should talk of one of these grey horrors remaining 'in the family' was fascinating.

"You've come to ask Viola about the attack on her, I suppose," said Stella resuming her patience.

"Attack?"

"You know what I mean. It was nearly an attack."

"Are you sure about that, Mrs. Whitehill?"

Stella looked up sharply.

"Sure? What else could it have been?"

"It could have been someone waiting in a car who realized he was causing anxiety to Miss Whitehill and wanted to reassure her."

"It could have been the Emperor of Ethiopia," retorted Stella tartly. "But it wasn't. It was the Stabber. There's not the slightest question about that."

Carolus looked at the bony, muscular-looking and rather unattractive woman. He could believe her capable of methodical charity if not spontaneous kindness but he found that he could not like her.

"Let's use our commonsense," she went on. "What ordinary man would be sitting in a car alone in Crabtree Avenue at that time in the evening, wearing a cloth cap, glasses and a raincoat? He would be asking for trouble, whoever he was. You don't seem to realize how people feel in this district. If a few of them had caught this man they would have been capable of . . ."

"Hanging him from a lamp-post?"

"Very nearly, I believe. Then, if he was the innocent you suppose . . ."

"Pardon me, I supposed nothing of the sort. I said he could have been someone waiting in a car."

"He wasn't. If you mean someone on legitimate business. As I was just going to say, *if* he was, why did he make off like that when Viola screamed?"

"You have answered that, Mrs. Whitehill. There was strong feeling among your neighbours. He could have suddenly realized what might be thought about him and done the wisest thing—decamped. That's exactly what I should have done in the circumstances."

This altercation was interrupted by Viola.

"You should have seen his eyes!" she said dramatically.

"What about them?" asked Carolus.

Viola seemed somewhat confused.

"They were glaring," she said, "*red* and glaring. The eyes of a murderer."

"Didn't you say he was wearing glasses?" asked Carolus mildly.

"Of course. *And* a cloth cap."

Carolus decided to leave it at that and turned again to Mrs. Whitehill. But before he could speak Viola said—"Don't forget I saw the knife, too."

Guessing that the knife would have become both vivid and circumstantial by this time Carolus again tried to leave the subject, but Mrs. Whitehill herself intervened.

"Yes, what about that?" she asked.

Carolus, driven into a corner, said—"It was very natural in the circumstances that Miss Whitehill should see something of the sort."

"You mean, I'm making it up?" cried Viola angrily.

"No. No. I mean it made itself up. You saw it all right, Miss Whitehill, but if the murders had been done by shooting you'd have seen a pistol, or if by strangling a noose."

"I'm not a complete fool," claimed Viola. "I saw the knife. I didn't imagine it."

"Whatever you saw won't help us much now," said Carolus pacifically. "What I wanted to ask you about, Mrs. Whitehill, was the night when Joyce Ribbing was murdered. The night of your Bridge party."

"Oh, that. There's nothing much to be said about that," said Stella Whitehill. "You know who was playing."

"Your husband was not at home?"

"My husband? What on earth's he got to do with it?"

"He wasn't in, anyway?"

"Certainly not. It was a Bridge four."

Carolus had to be satisfied with this somewhat ambiguous answer and said "Quite" in an encouraging voice.

"He came in about half an hour after Joyce had gone, as a matter of fact. In time for supper. Been down at the Mitre, of course. Where he is now."

Carolus felt it wiser to leave this aspect of the matter.

"When Joyce Ribbing left you that evening, Mrs. Whitehill, you did not feel the smallest anxiety about her going home alone?"

"Not the smallest. Why should we have, then?"

"There had been a brutal murder, after all, only a fortnight before, in this avenue, and no arrest had been made."

"One does not suppose, Mr. Whatever-your-name-is, that murders go in districts. If we thought about it at all we supposed that scmeone had reason to murder that schoolmistress. We did not suspect a maniac."

"I see."

"One swallow doesn't make a spring, you know," persisted Stella Whitehill, who had reached an impasse in her Patience and begun to cheat. "After the other two murders and Viola's narrow escape we knew where we stood. But not that night."

"Dr. Ribbing phoned about eleven?"

"Yes, and said Joyce wasn't home. Even then it did not occur to me till Viola suggested it."

"After you had left the phone?"

"Yes. About half an hour after. We were just going to bed when Viola remembered about the school-mistress and I phoned back to the doctor to hear if Joyce had come in. When I heard she hadn't I really did begin to wonder whether anything had happened."

"I was sure of it," said Viola almost ecstatically.

"Yes, my dear," said Stella harshly. "You were sure of it. But then *you* didn't know that Joyce Ribbing had a lover, and I did."

"Nothing else happened that evening to alarm you? Nothing after Joyce Ribbing left? You heard nothing from the street? I ask because this is one of the only houses in the avenue which hasn't got television."

"I won't have it," explained Stella Whitehill, adding a dismissal of the whole invention, "it's a bore. No, we heard nothing."

Carolus asked no more but rose to leave. As he was thanking the two women there was an interruption. A middle-aged man of medium height and commonplace features burst in, somewhat drunk.

"Don't tell him anything!" he said. "I've just been talking to the police. They say not to tell him anything."

"If you had told us that an hour ago . . ." began Stella.

"I've only just heard. I was talking to the police.

They said if he calls on us we're not to tell him anything." He turned to Carolus. "That's what they said," he added apologetically.

"I don't think you need worry," suggested Carolus gently.

"I don't worry," said Stella. "What use are the police, anyway? They haven't prevented these murders and here we are still living in conditions of siege. Neither Viola nor I can go out at night."

"I can, though," said Whitehill with a chuckle.

A storm was rising in Stella's square-set face and Carolus quickly took his leave. He did not envy Whitehill the next half hour.

He wanted to interview only two more people in this connection, but one at least of them would be difficult and painful—Dr. Ribbing. Until now he had witnessed nothing that could be called grief in this affair. Gerda Munshall had given the impression that she had taken up life again with renewed zest after the loss of her friend and Jim Crabbett had been philosophical, to say the least of it. But from Heatherwell and others Carolus had gathered that Ribbing was quite broken by his loss and he felt diffident about disturbing him with questions. However, he would try.

Whether or not Ribbing thought he was a patient Carolus could not decide, but he was shown to the doctor's consulting room. He briefly stated his business and was surprised to see the doctor nod and say he would tell Carolus all he could.

He was a little under average height and his face had a somewhat lugubrious expression which was not altogether the result of the tragedy, Carolus judged, but an expression of a morose character. He decided that as far as possible he would let the man say what he liked without more than prompting him here and there.

"These murders are the work of someone who has a certain knowledge of anatomy. They have been done with almost surgical skill, though considerable force was used."

"That is the quickest way to the heart, I believe?"

"That was the classical idea as certain sculptures show us. It has been used by suicides, I believe."

Carolus stared.

"Is it possible?"

"Quite, for a strong and determined man. Not, of course, that any of these murders could have been suicide."

"Would you say that the combination of knowledge, skill and force used in the first murder is sufficiently rare for us to be sure that the second murder was the work of the same person?"

"In my opinion, yes. It *is* possible, of course, that the second was the work of an imitator, but it is highly improbable. I believe that a homicidal maniac was responsible for all three."

"And that the maniac's choice of victims was entirely dictated by circumstances?"

"That seems obvious. If he was someone who would arouse no particular attention in Crabtree Avenue he could wait and watch till the circumstances combined. All he wanted was a dark night on which the weather would keep most people at home, a woman alone and no spectators. He could get these quite easily and did so twice within three weeks. As you can imagine, Mr. Deene, I have given a great deal of thought to this."

"What about the third murder?"

"Crabtree Avenue was under continuous observation. He had to go somewhere else."

"Why didn't he go to another district altogether? Wouldn't that have been safer?"

"My conclusion is that he was a resident here."

"Without transport then?"

"Probably. Another thing. All three of these women have been of less than average height. My wife was distinctly short. It may also be that the murderer had to add this to his conditions. If he himself was not tall it would be difficult to use that blow downward at the shoulder."

"Yes. I've thought of that. Do you suspect anyone, Doctor?"

The question came so swiftly and was so straight-aimed that Carolus himself was surprised at his own audacity.

Ribbing thought long before answering.

"I have no *reason* to suspect anyone," he said. "therefore I shall voice no suspicion of any individual. But it seems to me unlikely that it could be a stranger to the district . . ."

"Why? Since no one familiar was observed hanging about on any of the three nights in question, an unfamiliar person need not have been."

"I disagree. If the murderer was a resident in Crabtree Avenue he could have waited in his own house for a favourable time. And the fact that when he had to move his venue he chose another so near seems also to argue that he was a local. Personally I am convinced of it."

"So you suspect someone in this district of no more than average height whose movements cannot be accounted for on any of the three occasions?"

"Exactly. If I were investigating that is the way I would proceed."

"Very interesting, doctor. But you would come up against a snag at once. Who can account for his movements on three specific nights spread over several weeks? He may *think* he can, but unless he keeps a very detailed diary he would be in difficulties. Then you get alibis which may be honestly intended but are faked or self-convinced, a whole chaos of lies, conscious or unconscious."

"You have experience of these things and I have not. But I should have thought it possible to narrow it down."

"From what? There would be scores of people who would have to be considered. Do you, for instance, exclude the idea of a woman as the murderer?"

"Not altogether."

"Then where would one start? I tell you almost nobody could completely account for his movements on all three nights. Could you, for yours, for instance?"

"I could. In two cases I would have nothing that could be accepted as an alibi. The one alibi would exclude me from your list though."

"If nothing else did."

"Nothing else *would*," said Ribbing emphatically. "If, as we must suppose, these murders are the work of a schizophrenic nobody is excluded, not even those who have suffered by them. It will be circumstances and facts which will enable you to trace the man, not personality or characteristics. A schizophrenic homicide might be the mildest and most gentle man or woman so far as we know him."

"Would there be nothing in his everyday conduct to suggest an abnormal state of mind at certain times?"

"I am not an alienist. What little I have learnt of

psychiatry I have picked up as most G.P's do, in the course of my work. I think the symptoms are pretty varied. A tendency to isolation is one of them. There may be delusions of various sorts, silly beliefs and so on. Sudden excitement, too. Illogical thinking. Persecution mania. Delusions of grandeur. It's not very helpful. I tell you, I think you will only get your man by supposing he is sane, as he is most of the time."

"You don't think anyone could have had a motive?"

A grim smile moved Ribbing's tight lips.

"In all three cases?" he said. "No. I do not. Unless by motive you mean some obscure sub-human urge which may have actuated him. Certainly nothing which in a sane and normal mind could be a motive."

"Just old-fashioned blood-lust, in fact?"

"Yes."

Carolus saw that an expression of sadness and fatigue was deepening on the doctor's already gloomy face. He decided to ask no further questions but to get in touch with Turrell without mentioning him to the doctor. But he had a surprise.

"I suppose you intend to see Raymond Turrell?" Ribbing said.

"I must," said Carolus quietly.

"He's to be found in a pub called the Apple Tree in Chelsea most evenings at about seven, I understand."

"Thanks."

"He lives at 14 Rotterdam Street, Chelsea. His telephone number is Cheyne 2004," said Ribbing in a dull monotonous voice.

"You know him?"

"I've met him. He seems a very agreeable kind of man. And now, if you'll excuse me."

"I'm most grateful to you, doctor."

"I hope you're successful. Good night."

A very curious encounter, Carolus thought as he walked away from the house. Very curious indeed.

Thirteen

Carolus heard all he wanted from Turrell in half an hour in the Chelsea pub mentioned by Ribbing. They sat in a corner of the saloon in which there was too much of that fruity conversation laced with licentious wit of a kind common to the district. There were too many women with dogs, women dressed in popular versions of the season's designs, too many men with brush-like moustaches, and altogether too much brassy liveliness.

Turrell appeared to be the sort of man who belonged to this. He had not a moustache but he dressed the part, wore a regimental tie, and spoke in a rich plummy voice.

"But I don't *quite* understand," he said when Carolus had introduced himself, "why you come to me."

"You were a friend of Joyce Ribbing's, I believe."

"I knew her. But what's that got to do with it? She was murdered by a maniac."

"I am trying to find out a little about each of the victims."

"Very praiseworthy, I'm sure, but quite useless. How can it possibly help you to identify the murderer?"

"I don't know that it will. But it might, and there's not much else I can do."

"You might try to prevent another woman being murdered," said Turrell with a touch of bitterness.

"I don't think another woman will be murdered," said Carolus.

"So you've got a theory?"

"The beginnings of one."

"And you think I can help you to build it up?"

"It's possible."

"It all sounds rather forlorn to me. I've nothing to hide, of course. Every blasted Tom, Dick and Harry seems to know that we were having an affair. Even newspapers have practically said so. If you want me to tell you it's true I'll do so."

Carolus hesitated.

"I think I understand how you feel," he said at last. "It's hateful to have one's private life discussed all over the place. You must naturally think that your feelings for Joyce, and hers for you, are your own affair. I wasn't, believe me, trying to intrude on them."

Then Carolus had one of those surprises which occasionally came to him from the middle of conversation. Looking at his glass and speaking very quietly, Turrell said, "I loved her." He might almost have said "I killed her," so unexpected was the simple statement.

"And she?" said Carolus.

"No. I'm afraid not. Or not enough. She had made it quite clear to me that she wouldn't leave her husband. I could never shake her on that though God knows I tried."

Carolus waited.

"It wasn't money," went on Turrell. "I have an income. Nothing enormous but probably a good deal more than Ribbing earned. And she had money. It wasn't her home, either. She loathed that ghastly suburb. And it wasn't that she was in love with Ribbing. It was just loyalty and—if you like—decency. She was what used to be called straight. Oh, I know we had an affair. But she would never let it interfere with her . . . home life."

Without a word Turrell took their two glasses to the counter and came back with them filled.

"You don't want to intrude, you say," he continued. "Then perhaps you've got more than you bargained for. I've told you a few home truths. Or wasn't that what you wanted? Were you going to ask me where I was on the night of the crime?"

"No. I wasn't going to ask you that," said Carolus.

"The police did, believe it or not."

"Could you tell them?"

"Yes. I was here till closing time, fortunately. Getting drunk."

"And on the other nights?"

"What other nights?" asked Turrell rather vacantly.

"If the police were logical, after asking you about your movements on the night of Joyce Ribbing's murder they would have gone on to the other two murders."

"I never thought of that. They didn't, though. It wouldn't have been much use. I've no idea where I was. At a show, perhaps. Or a party."

"You weren't in Albert Park, anyway," said Carolus, not letting it sound like a query.

"I've never been in Albert Park in my life. I suppose I've been somewhere near it on my way out of London.

Not far from Lewisham, isn't it? But to my knowledge I've never even been through it."

"And of course you knew no one connected with the place except Joyce Ribbing."

"I've met her husband, since. Otherwise no one at all."

"You say you've driven through Lewisham. You have a car?"

"An old Jag. Why?"

Carolus looked rather uncomfortable, but turned the question to motoring, which absorbed them both for another five minutes, till Carolus left.

He felt greatly dispirited. His personal enquiries were finished and had brought him no nearer to certainty. It was true that if his theory could be made to hold water no other woman would be stabbed in Albert Park, but he had no measuring proof behind it and only the most circumstantial of evidence. Besides, even his theory did not mean that there would not be another murder and Heatherwell was a perpetual anxiety to him.

When he reached Crabtree Avenue it was between eight and nine o'clock, the time, approximately, at which all three murders had been committed. It was a gusty dark night and the street was deserted. Passing number 32 he continued up the slope till he reached the trees opposite the school gates among which the wife of the school caretaker thought she had seen someone move on the night of the first murder.

Carolus stood there a moment watching the empty street. A group of three left one of the houses near Perth Avenue and walked towards the lights of Inverness Road. Two boys could be seen on the pavement barging into one another playfully before they turned into one of the houses in the lower part of the avenue. Otherwise Carolus could see no one.

But that did not mean the street was wholly deserted. In any one of those front gardens someone could be waiting, as someone had waited in all probability, at least on the night of the second murder.

Suddenly, standing there, Carolus had a sense of identity with the murderer, as though something in his sub-conscious mind responded to the macabre impulses which had driven him out to kill. It was as though he understood those impulses, as though he too could start forward when a woman came out of the school gates alone, could follow her down the footpath and understand the mad excitement of plunging the knife downward. Deliberately mesmerizing himself into this, he stooped over the corpse in his mind, picked up the dead body and concealed it under the hedge. He almost felt the psychotic exaltation of the moment. But a few minutes later the reaction came flooding in and he looked down at his hands in horror as though to see if they were bloody.

That was it. The reaction. Within hours, perhaps within minutes of the act the murderer must have felt this exhausting disgust with himself and what he had done. More likely minutes—while he yet stood on the pavement outside the garden where the body lay. He would loathe not only the thought of that corpse but of himself, of his mania, of his brutality. Apart from the danger of being where he was he would feel the horror of being alone, he would look with longing at the lights of Inverness Road where ordinary people went cheerfully about their business.

As Carolus looked down Crabtree Avenue as though with the eyes of the murderer, he saw the bright lights of the Mitre at its foot. So must the murderer have looked, and in looking have longed to be among other men drinking there. How better face this dreary and grim reaction? To hear voices, to drink cheerfully, to be surrounded by normal contented people, it must have drawn him irresistibly. Perhaps, if he *was* a local, some of them would be known to him. What more reassuring than to be greeted as he entered? Out of the blackness in which he had been astray, out of the night of sick fancies and maniacal violence, he could come to his own kind, to people who knew him and would never connect him with the demonic events of the night.

But how could he enter the Mitre? Impossible to have struck that blow without some bloodstains. Perhaps his coat . . . perhaps . . .

Carolus began to walk down Crabtree Avenue at a fast pace. That was it! A hope, anyway. For at the foot of Oaktree Avenue, on the far side of the park and opposite to the park-keeper's lodge, there was a prominent notice *Public Conveniences*. These were so constructed that sexual segregation began at the top of two separate staircases, euphemistically marked *Ladies* and *Gentlemen*. Did this useful institution contain an attendant? Did it supply its clients with a *Wash and Brush-up*? Was there running hot water? If the answer to all these was affirmative, Carolus might be on the verge of something more definite.

He hurried along Inverness Road and reached his objective. Yes, there was an attendant. Yes, there were wash-basins. As Carolus gazed round him he felt himself scrutinized by the attendant, a bad-tempered-looking gnome with an old pair of spectacles repaired with sticking-plaster who pulled at an empty pipe.

"Evening," said Carolus.

"Um," said the attendant curtly.

"I should like a few words with you. But perhaps you're tired of answering questions."

"What about?"

Straight to the point, thought Carolus.

"About the night of the murders."

The attendant blinked.

"Come in here," he commanded, indicating his tiled den. "You may believe it or not," he began impressively, "but do you know not one single soul has been to ask me anything about it? It's not to be credited, is it? All those police paid out of the taxpayer's money and not one of them been near me? It's enough to make you weep. With all I've seen and know about it, there hasn't been a soul come to me ever since it happened."

"You didn't think of reporting what you knew?"

"Not me. If they can't trouble to come to me, I thought, it's not likely I'm going traipsing up to see them. They'll wake up to it sooner or later, I said, then they won't half be sorry they didn't think of it earlier."

"Perhaps, yes."

"It isn't as though they don't come down here. There's two of them in plain clothes up and down every night watching for Goings On, I suppose. As if I wasn't able to stop any Goings On there might be. I know my job. I very soon tell them, if I see any of that. Not that I'd get them in trouble like these two I was telling you about want to do. But I won't have any of that in my Convenience . . ."

"You were saying you noticed . . ."

"Yes. I did. I've got eyes in my head. I shouldn't be surprised if what I noticed on the two nights of those first murders wouldn't be enough to tell anyone straight away who done them. Only not a single solitary blind soul's been to ask me about it."

"I have," said Carolus.

"Yes, but you're not the police. What I thought, what anyone would have thought, was that the police would be down the very day after it happened. But no. I might as well have been blind and deaf and dumb so far as they're concerned. And the papers are just as bad. You'd have thought .they'd have wanted to put my picture in the papers five or six times over for what I could tell them. But not one has ever set foot in the place to ask me. It makes you think, doesn't it?"

"It certainly does," said Carolus inevitably.

"I don't see how I can tell you," regretted the attendance. "It's the police ought to have asked me. If I go and tell you I shan't hear no more about it and there I shall be. I might as well have not noticed anything."

"What is it you want?" asked Carolus.

"Well, I could do with something, couldn't I, after all that trouble? Then again you'd think the papers would send someone. I've never been a witness in anything like a case before. The police don't like it that they've never had anyone up for Goings On in my convenience. They don't like that at all. They used to send a young chap down to try and start something and then grab them but I wouldn't have that. 'No Goings On', I'd say before he'd had time to get anyone into trouble. So I've never been a witness."

Carolus tried a five-pound note.

"Much obliged," said the attendant, putting it away, "only I did think the newspapers . . ."

"If your information leads to anything I've no doubt

the papers will be interested," said Carolus rather pompously. "What did you see?"

"It wasn't Goings On, or anything like that," said the attendant. "Nor yet it wasn't anyone giving trouble which I often do have, when they've had a few. It was just this man."

Carolus could not help it. "Which man?" he asked.

"This man who came in here just after each of the first two murders and had never been in before or since."

"How do you know it was just after the murders?"

"It said what the times was in the papers, didn't it? Must have been just after. I close at ten and it wasn't long before I closed. Only the first time it was earlier than the second, same as the murder was, so it said in the papers."

"What about this man?"

"What about him? He was the murderer, of course."

"Why? Was he wearing a cloth cap, glasses and a raincoat?"

"No he wasn't. That's what makes me think. He'd taken them off."

"How do you know that?"

"Well it stands to reason, doesn't it? Here's a man in the depths of winter coming down here without a hat or a coat. What else could it have been?"

"I see your point. What more did you notice about him?"

"What didn't I? It's not many wants a wash-basin and towel at that time of night, but he did. You should have seen the way he washed. Taking his time over it. Then when he's not washing any more he's standing looking at himself in the glass till I thought he'd drive me out of my mind. This way, that way, looking at his sleeves and his trousers. All I can say is if he hadn't just done those murders I don't know who had."

"Nor do I," admitted Carolus. "What did he look like?"

"Just like anyone else," said the attendant disappointingly. "Bout your height only older than what you are. In his forties, I daresay. Or perhaps his fifties. Nothing much to notice about him. Dressed quiet. Nothing to call the attention."

"You are sure you'd never seen him before?"

"Well if I had he must have slipped in here and out again when I wasn't looking. Some of them do do that."

"You know many of the local residents by sight?"

"I daresay I do. You get to, in this job. Only I don't know their names."

"You know the park-keeper opposite?"

"Jack Slatter? Course I do. Known him for years."

"Was the man who came here on those two nights anything like him?"

"Like Jack? Now that you mention it you're not far off. It wasn't him, of course, but much the same style of man. Only better got up, if you know what I mean."

"You say this man was here some time?"

"Must have been. All that washing and looking at himself in the mirror and examining his clothes."

"How long would you say?"

"Five minutes or so. May have been no more than four. There was people coming and going all the time."

"Do you think he knew you were watching him?"

"No, I don't. I can keep an eye on anyone without their knowing anything about it. You have to in this job."

"Did he seem upset about anything?"

"Calm as a cucumber. That's what they say about

those that do murders. They don't turn a hair."

"Would you know him if you saw him again?"

"Know him? Certainly I should. Pick him out anywhere. That's what the police ought to have done. Had an identification parade. I'd have spotted him all right. It isn't as though he'd only come in the once. Twice, he was here. Each time just after a murder."

"But not after the third murder," pondered Carolus.

"Stands to reason, doesn't it? He wasn't going to do that. Not the third time, with everybody looking for him. Though for all the police know or care he might have done. Fancy their not even coming to ask me. It passes belief, doesn't it? They can dress up and come down here trying to get a case against someone for Goings On, but they can't come and ask a simple question when anyone knows something."

"I think you should report what you know to them."

"Me? What do you take me for? Let them do the asking. I'm not holding back anything. But I can't speak if I'm not asked, can I?"

"Yes," said Carolus. "You could go to the detective in charge of the case and tell him what you know. It's your duty to do so."

"Duty? It's my duty to keep this Convenience clean and tidy and see there's no Goings On, that's all. It's their duty to catch this Stabber they talk about. Though I must say he didn't look much like a stabber. Too quiet and well-behaved, I should have thought, for any lark like that. Though you can't tell."

"Why do you think he came here?" asked Carolus curiously.

"It's obvious, isn't it? He wanted to make sure there was no blood on him before . . ."

"Before what?"

"Suppose he had to go somewhere where there was people. To fix his alibi and that. Well, he couldn't go if he had bloodstains all over his clothes, could he? Or on his hands."

"And had he?"

"I'm not to know, am I? I couldn't go and watch him all the time. I didn't actually see any bloodstains. I'll admit that. But there must have been. You can't stab someone to death and drop them in the garden without getting blood on you."

"And you're sure you'd know him? If I were to come down here with him one day, you'd be able to tell me afterwards?"

"Yes. I've told you I should. Couldn't mistake him."

"Perhaps I will," said Carolus.

"Mean to say you know him?"

"I know a lot about him," said Carolus, "and you've helped me considerably. I'm glad I thought of coming to you."

"That's all right. Only it's past talking about that the police didn't do it weeks ago."

"One other thing I'd like to ask you. If you'd met this man in the Mitre . . ."

"I'm strictly T.T.", said the attendant. "Never been in the Mitre in my life and never shall. Or any other place selling alcoholic refreshment," he added unctuously.

"Good-night," returned Carolus.

Carolus at last escaped from the attendant's tiled cubby-hole and with some relief ascended to the windy air of Inverness Road.

Fourteen

NEXT morning, a Sunday, Carolus woke to find one of those freakishly warm days which occasionally happen in the spring and cause English people to walk about saying "we shall have to pay for this". It reminded him of one area of the suburb he had not yet explored, Albert Park itself, that railed-off plot of trees and grass from which the whole district took its name. He decided to spend a few hours there and taking *The Sunday Times* and *The Observer*, folded to expose Mephisto and Ximenes respectively, he set out, reaching the gates by the lodge as a harsh little bell stopped ringing in the Victorian gothic steeple of St. Luke's down the road.

Near the lodge gates he saw the park-keeper in uniform. Here was another man of medium height and Carolus began to ask himself when, in this case, he would find someone really tall or short, someone obviously excluded from Miss Pilkin's description of the man she had seen hanging about in Salisbury Gardens before the third murder—"of average height or perhaps a little smaller."

Slatter *was* of average height but so was every other male in the district or connected with the murdered women. Or so it seemed.

Carolus said good morning to Slatter as he passed to receive a nod and half-smile in return. But the weather was so splendid after the long misery of winter that Slatter could not resist adding—"Lovely morning, isn't it?"

Carolus had no intention of questioning the park-keeper at this time but he wanted to know something of the man and said—"Yes. Lovely. You've a fine show of spring bulbs."

This was not strictly true of the few sooty daffodils visible from where Carolus stood, but it seemed to please Slatter.

"I like to see a few nice daffs," he said smiling proudly.

"What do you think of all these murders?" asked Carolus in a chatty way.

"Dreadful," said Slatter with conventional solemnity. "Dreadful thing. And I'm right in the middle of it, as you might say."

"So you are. You live here, I suppose?"

"That's my little place," said Slatter indicating the stucco lodge.

"Convenient," remarked Carolus. "Not damp, is it?"

"Dry as a bone and I should know because I used to get rheumatism when I was in the army and I've never had so much as a twinge of it since I came here. No. My trouble is I can't sleep."

"Can't sleep?"

"Very seldom. Insomnia, they call it. I've got it terribly bad. I've tried everything to cure it, but nothing seems to do much good. If I sleep a couple of hours in a night I'm lucky."

"That's bad," said Carolus.

"It *is* bad. Someone tried to tell me it was cheese caused it. I always eat a bit of bread and cheese before turning in. So I knocked it off for a few nights. But it didn't do a bit of good. I soon went back to it and never been without it again. But I still can't sleep."

"I don't envy you. All alone, are you?"

"Yes. I don't mind that part of it. I've lived alone for nearly twenty years now since my wife was Taken. It's being right in the middle of it all I don't like and having the police round asking questions."

"That must be annoying."

"It seems I could have done them—all three of them," explained Slatter rather too jovially, Carolus thought. "There's not many placed as I am between them. And living alone I've got no one to say where I was those nights."

"But surely . . ."

"I don't say they actually suspect me but they asked questions about where I was and that. It's not very nice, is it?"

"It's not at all nice. The whole thing's unpleasant. Have you told many people about your being questioned?"

"I've made no secret of it. I've got nothing to be ashamed of."

"Then don't let anyone into your lodge at night," said Carolus with sudden vehemence. "Not even someone you know."

Slatter stared at him.

"Whatever's come over you?" he asked.

"I mean what I say," said Carolus. "Don't take any chances about this. Keep your door locked."

"Well I don't know," said the astounded Slatter.

"And who might you be to tell me anything like that? You're not from the police, are you?"

"It doesn't matter who I am," said Carolus. "Take a warning when you get one."

"I don't know what to think. First the police asking questions then you as good as telling me the Stabber's after me. It doesn't seem to make sense. Don't I have enough troubles as it is, trying to stop the kids trampling on the flower beds and see people keep their dogs on the lead?"

Slatter looked thoroughly baffled. He had a good-natured face, set now in lines of perplexity.

"I can only beg you to listen to what I told you," Carolus said, and nodding curtly walked on to find a seat.

In spite of the gay spring weather he thought the park a dismal place of asphalt paths, weedy grass and geometrical beds and the people of the district more than usually unpicturesque in their Sunday clothes. He found a place from which the lodge and gates at the exit to Inverness Road were visible. Since Slatter continued to wait about in that region, apparently having a kindly word for most of those who entered, he too remained in sight.

Presently a familiar figure appeared. Outsize and awkward in a coat and skirt, the calves of her legs formidable over her square-toed shoes, Grace Buller strode in. She stopped to chat with Slatter for a moment and as both of them took side glances at him he gathered that Slatter was giving the gist of their recent conversation.

Carolus felt impotent and alarmed. There were some people who could not keep their mouths shut, whatever was at stake.

Grace Buller strode straight up to Carolus.

"Hullo," she said. "What do you want to scare poor old Slatter for?"

"Good morning," said Carolus. "I remember you told me Slatter was 'a dear old man'. I suppose he's quite a friend of yours?"

"Oh, we're great friends. I play tennis here in the summer and he always manages to give me a court."

"So you come to see him even in the holidays from . . . where is it you live, Miss Buller?"

"Woolwich, actually. But I often come this way."

"On the scooter?"

"When I can get it to start," said Grace Buller with a broad smile. "I came on it this morning. Went like a bomb."

"Good. When does your term start again?"

"Tomorrow week. We always go back on a Monday. I don't know what it'll be like next term. I'm sure half the parents will take their children away. Unless the Stabber's caught in the meantime, that is. You can't blame them, can you?"

"I suppose not."

"Well, I must be off. I usually walk a couple of times round the park on Sundays. Training, you see. Bye."

She strode manfully away and Carolus welcomed this for he had just seen another group enter of people he knew—the Goggins and a man whom Heatherwell had pointed out to him as Tuckman. They did no more than nod to Slatter and when they had settled on a seat some two hundred yards away from him, Carolus walked across.

He was introduced to Tuckman, a talkative, opinionated character who at once launched into a dissertation on the murders while Ada Goggins sustained herself with cakes from a paper bag.

"What you've got to look for," he told Carolus, "is someone suffering from one of the various mental disorders which produce murderers. Persecution mania, for instance. If someone is going about with the belief that an enemy is trying to kill him he may strike back. In this case it would be someone who believes his life is threatened by a small woman living in Albert Park. So he would look for such people and strike."

"Quite," said Carolus who did not want to interrupt Tuckman.

"Delusions of grandeur could account for these murders, too. A man or a woman suffering from them might see his victims as interfering with his aims. If Crabtree Avenue was, in his disordered imagination, his domain he would be merely ordering to the executioner those who interrupted his reveries."

"Just so."

"One type of epileptic may commit murder during a seizure and have complete amnesia afterwards. I wonder how much attention you or the police have given to this possibility. If I were in charge of the case the first person I should look for would be an epileptic."

"Do you know any in the district?" asked Carolus.

"No. But surely Ribbing could help there. Then, of course, there's sadism."

"What's that exactly?" asked Ada Goggins with her mouth full.

"It is a sex perversion centring round cruelty," Tuckman explained, "which takes its name from the Marquis de Sade. No wonder you ask—the word is greatly abused. But sadism has accounted for some of history's most gruesome murders and the three we are discussing bear all the marks of sadism."

"So all we have to do is to find a paranoiac, an epileptic or a sadist who was in Crabtree Avenue or Salisbury Gardens on the three occasions?" suggested Carolus who, like most schoolmasters, disliked being lectured.

"That's it," said Tuckman. "I wonder you haven't found him already. I think we in the district have played our part. Our volunteer force has probably prevented several more attacks. We shan't relax our vigilance till the Stabber has been identified."

"He may never be," said Carolus.

"He will. You can be sure of that. He's bound to strike again and then we shall have him."

"So you're counting on that?" said Carolus.

"We hope to prevent it, of course. Our vigilante force is quite large now and drawn from the whole district. Of course if he leaves the area altogether and breaks out somewhere else there's nothing we can do. But I don't think he will."

"Seen that tall woman again, Mr. Goggins?" asked Carolus suddenly.

"I'm not sure," said Goggins. "I thought, the other evening, I saw someone uncommonly like her come out of Perth Avenue and turn up Crabtree Avenue, but when I looked again she had disappeared."

"I think he imagined it," said Ada Goggins screwing up her empty paper bag. "Come along. We must get home to lunch."

Carolus returned to his place for an opening attack on Mephisto whom he found more than usually capricious and illogical. 'Grooms are stumped when in suitable roles'—ostlers was obviously the answer—but why should 'a little dog making the maximum sound' be 'Peke', as it was obviously intended to be? Obscurity was one thing, sheer facetiousness in the setter was unforgivable.

Just then he looked up and saw, sailing down the asphalt like a schooner, none other than Miss Pilkin with Ursus firmly held on a lead. He rose and raised his hat. Miss Pilkin peered at him a moment.

"Ah yes," she said. "The young man who asked me those intelligent questions about my dangerous neighbours. You've met Ursus, haven't you? Yes, I see he recognizes you."

Carolus made suitable small talk for a time then ventured to enquire about the Pressleys. Miss Pilkin answered readily.

"There is trouble about the Will," she said. "There always is in a family of that kind."

"How do you know?"

"The father, from Bromley, arrived the other night bringing his late wife's solicitor with him. At least I presume it was his wife's. A local solicitor, anyway. My excellent tenants recognized him, having employed him to draw up some document for them. The family opposite went into a long conference from which the man Pressley emerged first, in a towering rage."

"I can't help wondering how you knew he was in a towering rage," said Carolus admiringly.

"When a man turns back at the door to shout something unmentionable to those inside, then slams the door, then strides off down the street he may surely be considered to be in a rage. Later he was followed, with a little more dignity, by Crabbett and the solicitor. I do not of course know what was decided about the Will," added Miss Pilkin regretfully."

"Or even if a Will was discussed."

"Of that I am certain. My instincts never mislead

me. Some sordid dispute was doubtless going on."

"You have noticed nothing else of significance?"

"Isn't that enough?" asked Miss Pilkin dramatically. Then, gazing full into Carolus's eyes she said—"And you, Mr. Deene, what have *you* noticed of significance? What progress have you made towards the apprehension of this murderer?"

"Not enough," said Carolus. "I've collected a lot of circumstantial evidence."

"Don't lose courage. Stick to it, Mr. Deene. For all my deepest intuitions tell me that *you're getting warm!*"

"I beg your pardon?"

"You're on the right track! I knew you would find the truth as soon as I saw you. You were so quick to understand the infamy of the family living opposite to me. You have perceptions—not perhaps as keen as mine but still quick and sure enough to guide you. Ursus knows this, too. Don't you, Ursus?" As if she had just realized this discourtesy of leaving someone out of a conversation, she now gave her full attention to the dog, speaking of and to him, fortunately, in adult terms. "Yes, he knows perfectly well, he says, that you will get at the truth. He's a little impatient just now because we're going to a lawn at the far end of the park, out of sight of Mr. Slatter, where Ursus can throw off his inhibitions with his lead. 'Come *along*,' he says, and I must go. Farewell, Mr. Deene. May you soon be successful."

She sailed on.

As Carolus was about to leave the park he was intercepted by Slatter.

"I should like to know what you meant by telling what you did this morning."

Carolus looked closely at him and saw that in spite of

his genial expression there was a hard glitter in the eyes.

"Exactly what I said. I think you are in some danger."

"What kind of danger? From the police, d'you mean?"

"That too, for all I know."

"You talked as though it was from the Stabber. Telling me to lock my door, and that."

"Do you often go to the Mitre?"

"Yes, I do. And why not?"

"No reason at all. It's quite a meeting place, I gather."

"There's a good few get in the saloon most evenings," explained Slatter.

"And you have mentioned there that you were questioned by the police?"

"I daresay I have."

"And said what you said to me, that so far as circumstances are concerned you could have been guilty of all three murders?"

"What about it?"

"It may be nothing. I may be wrong. But there's no harm in taking precautions."

"I don't see it," said Slatter obstinately. "If there was any danger the police would know of it."

"The police know only one kind of danger," said Carolus.

"Now look here," said Slatter. "I don't know who you are or what it's got to do with you. But I'm not a fool—nor one to be scared by a lot of talk just because there's a madman about who stabs women. I was thirty years in the army before I got this job."

"Really? What regiment?"

"RASC, if you want to know. I was a sergeant. If you think I'm going to be put out now by talk of hidden danger you're mistaken. I shall go on now as I've always gone. I've never locked my door at night and I shan't now."

"Then I can only hope I'm mistaken," said Carolus and walked away.

He decided to lunch at the Golden Cockerel, to escape from Albert Park for a few hours. The fine weather seemed only to emphasize the drab respectability of the place and sunlight on the asphalt paths and struggling evergreens of the park was depressing. In the streets was an overpowering smell of Sunday dinners being cooked.

He found at the Golden Cockerel a note left for him by Miss Cratchley, the headmistress of St. Olave's Ladies College. She had phoned twice and called to see him but the staff had been unable to tell her where Carolus was. The note asked simply that Carolus should get in touch with her as soon as possible.

There was nothing for it now but a visit to the Mitre. He had a queer sense of climax as he decided this, as if he knew that it would bring him, if not to certainty, at least to a resolution of his most pressing doubts.

Fifteen

CAROLUS reached the Mitre on the stroke of opening time as many a customer, for no less urgent-seeming though for different reasons, must have done before him. He found the landlord alone behind the bar, a bald blue-chinned man with a narrow head and an alert manner.

Carolus decided to take advantage of his momentary lead over the other customers to put his case squarely and swiftly to the man, whose name he had learnt from the licensee's notice over the door was John Samuel Chumside. He did so and felt the landlord's keen glance on him.

"You see," Carolus ended, "the Mitre's right at the centre of all this. I've found when I've investigated cases before that I can learn more in the local than anywhere else."

"I daresay," said Chumside.

"And in this case, particularly, almost every man in any way connected with the murdered women seems to use this house, as well as many of the inhabitants of Crabtree Avenue."

"Only natural, isn't it? Being handy like it is. But its been a dam' nuisance for me, all this business. Gives the district a bad name, having this Stabber prowling around. Upsets my regulars."

"Three women have been killed, Mr. Chumside," said Carolus with a touch of severity.

"I know. I know. Three of them have been stabbed and maybe more to come. I was only saying it upset things. I'd be the first to want the man caught and put a stop to."

"Then you'll give me what information you can?"

"It depends what you want."

"I don't know that yet. I'm working on a hunch very largely. But I'd like to feel you'll help me if you can. You're in a unique position to know people's movements."

"Well, I am and I'm not. For instance, very few women ever come in here. I don't know how it is but there are pubs that get that, especially in districts like this. The King's Head's full of women. Just up the top of the park, that is. They all take their wives in there. But not in this house. The men seem to like the saloon to themselves and it becomes a sort of habit. You'll see that for yourself presently." Chumside paused. "All right," he said at last. "I don't mind telling you anything I've noticed if it's going to help to get this business out of the way."

He was called away to serve and Carolus waited impatiently.

"It's a bit more complicated than you think," he said when the landlord returned. "And I don't quite see how a busy man like you is going to have time to notice all I want."

As so often happens, a challenge of this kind was accepted eagerly.

"Why not?" said Chumside. "The wife will be down in a minute and there's Fred who helps us out on Sundays as well as Laura who comes on late this evening because she likes to go to church. But she'll be here very soon. I can watch out for what you want."

"I don't want to be here myself. Too many know of my interest in the case. Would it be possible for me to see you after closing time?"

"Come round the back," said Chumside. "And don't let the Law see you. They're always standing about on the dot at ten. Now who is it you want to know about?"

"You mustn't suppose that these are necessarily suspects," said Carolus. "I'm afraid there are quite a few."

"Go on, then," said Chumside.

"First you know Slatter the park-keeper?"

"Old Jack? Certainly I do."

"Then from the avenue itself Goggins?"

"Yerss."

"Tuckman?"

Chumside nodded.

"Young Gates?"

"Yes. What about his old man? He must be nearly eighty," said Chumside.

Carolus shook his head. "But there's Whitehill," he added. "And Turnwright."

"I know both of them."

"Heatherwell?"

"He doesn't often come in but I know who you mean."

"There's a man named Crabbett who comes from Bromley. His wife was one of the victims."

"I've only known who it was since it happened. He

used to come in from time to time—perhaps once a week. But since his wife died its most nights. What about Reg Titchcock, the caretaker from the school?"

"All right," conceded Carolus. "That's about all. What I chiefly want to know is who talks with whom, if there are any serious conversations going on."

"You shall."

"And anything else you notice. This is very good of you, Mr. Chumside."

"That's all right. It suits me to get it out of the way, too. The Law don't seem to be getting anywhere."

"Oh, does the doctor ever come in?"

"Who? Ribbing? Now and again on Sunday, he does."

"Add him to your list then. And I suppose you don't know . . . how could you, though . . ."

"Who's that?" asked the landlord sharply.

"The first woman to be killed had a brother. An actor who rides a motor-bike."

"No. I don't know him," said Chumside regretfully. "Live here, does he?"

"No. Blackheath."

"Not likely to come in here then."

"I thought he might have come over for his sister, perhaps."

"Not that I know of. She never came in here, anyway. Not according to her picture in the papers. That's the lot then?"

"Yes."

"Nice little job you're giving me but I'll do what I can. You've chosen a good night, Sunday."

"It's not only tonight, I'm afraid. Next week as well."

"We must see," promised Chumside turning away to serve another customer.

Carolus had not seen Heatherwell that day but when he reached number 32 he did not find him. Gone to the Mitre, he supposed.

He returned to the Mitre at 10:15 as he had been instructed and knocked at the back door. He soon found that Chumside had entered all too fully into the secrecy and drama of his role for after Carolus had waited some minutes the door opened ajar.

"Is the Law around?" Chumside asked.

"No."

"All right. Come in. Don't make a noise. The wife has gone to bed."

They went to a small bare room.

"Well, we *have* had a night of it," said Chumside enjoyably when they were settled. "Nearly all the lot in and that Heatherwell carrying on like a lunatic."

"I'm afraid he's not very well-balanced," said Carolus.

"Balanced? He's off his rocker. He hadn't even had a drink this evening, or not more than one or two, when he started."

"Started what?"

"Started talking about doing for himself and I don't know what not. If you ask my opinion he's not all there. One minute he was laughing at the top of his voice and the next he was telling someone he wished he was dead. That's no way to talk on licensed premises. I had to tell him in the end. 'Don't start talking like that in here, Mr. Heatherwell', I said. 'Because I don't like it and my customers don't like it either'. He shut up a bit after that."

"Did he say anything about his wife?"

"Yes. His wife had left him. He was all alone. All that."

"No one at his house?"

"No. That was what was worrying him."

"What time did he leave?"

"Not till just before closing time. He seemed to have calmed down a bit then."

"Who else was in?"

"That Goggins came in as he very often does. Doesn't say a lot but when he does its like a judge talking. And Tuckman who was laying down the law of course. On about what the police ought to be doing to catch this Stabber which I didn't think very nice with Jim Crabbett, whose wife was murdered, sitting there listening. But that Tuckman's one of them who always knows."

"Was the doctor in?"

"No. He didn't come in this evening. But Slatter from the park was here."

"Did he say I talked to him this morning?"

"No. He was talking again about his not being able to sleep. It's not the first time, either. He's tried everything for it, he says. He puts it down to something he got in the war. He doesn't half go on about it."

"He's another one who lives alone, isn't he?"

"Yes. Seems there's something to be said for married life, after all, doesn't it? Old Jack's lived alone in that little lodge ever since he came here. Doesn't even have anyone to tidy up for him. I tell you who was here tonight, though. That Turnwright. He's the one who wouldn't have anything to do with these Vigilantes when they was formed. He's a funny chap, Turnwright. Very funny. The way he talks about these murders. Thank goodness the doctor wasn't here and Crabbett had gone when he began. 'I hope this Stabber hasn't finished before he gets my old woman', he said. 'I tell her to take a walk every evening about eight or nine on the off-chance, but there's no luck so far.' Of course it's only talk. I couldn't help smiling but the wife said I ought to be ashamed of myself. He's a character, really."

"Did Whitehill come in?"

"I believe he did for a minute. You scarcely know whether he's in or out. He doesn't say anything. Just enjoys his one or two gin-and-ginger ales. But I'll tell you who *was* in tonight. That Titchcock from up at the girls' school. He'd got plenty to say for himself, as usual. But nothing on The Subject."

"What about young Gates?"

"I haven't seen him all the evening. There was others, of course. We've been very busy. But no more on your list. One or two women, tonight. With their husbands, that is."

"I never asked you before," said Carolus. "But do you get a man called Pressley in. From Salisbury Gardens?"

"Used to do," said Chumside. "But I haven't seen him for a long time now. Someone told me he'd started going to the King's Head. Well, its nearer for him, I suppose. No, there's nothing more I can tell you tonight."

"There were no intense conversations?"

"Not really. They seemed to sit round, if you know what I mean, tonight. Slatter had a few words with Goggins over on one side. I believe Whitehill and Heatherwell were together for a moment. But nothing to notice."

"Thank you very much, Mr. Chumside. You've been very helpful. I really think I'm getting somewhere and what you have told me is truly important. It may even be a matter of life and death. May I come and see you tomorrow?"

"Yes. We don't close till eleven, though."

At number 32 Carolus found Heatherwell perfectly sound and calm.

"I rather lost my head tonight," he told Carolus.

"Yes. In the Mitre."

"So you know."

"It's my business to know what goes on. That's why I've come to stay here."

"I don't know what made me go off the deep end tonight. I really don't. I'd scarcely had a drink."

Carolus refrained from expressed sympathy or concern for several reasons, one of which was that they might bring floods more psychotic confidences. He contented himself by saying—"Do you have any trouble with sleeping?"

"It's funny you should ask that," said Heatherwell. "You'd think I would have, wouldn't you? All that tension and everything. But not a bit. I usually sleep like a log."

Carolus envied him. Lately he had been lying awake for hours before he slept. The case was worrying him far more than any other. He was oppressed by his inability to do anything decisive quickly enough. He and the police seemed almost to be waiting for the murderer to strike again.

But tonight he felt exhausted and sleep came, though fitfully at first, soon after he had got into bed, certainly before midnight.

Then suddenly he was awake. He was aware of the curious fact that he knew what had awakened him though he had not consciously heard the sound. Someone had rung the front-door bell.

Carolus moved swiftly and silently. He pulled on a dressing-gown and a pair of soft bedroom slippers. He was glad that he had never used those sloppy things with backs trodden down in which one could not move fast without noise. He glanced at his watch, 12:25.

The house seemed very still. Carolus gently turned the handle of his door and opened it a crack. Everything was silence.

Again the bell rang. This time it brought sounds of hurried movements from Heatherwell's room. Loud sounds of movements, too. Heatherwell was evidently not trying to be quiet. It was almost as though there was something hysterical in the way he moved about. His door burst open and Carolus heard the flap-flap of his slippers as he sped downstairs. There were sounds of a chain being taken off and bolts pulled back then the door opened.

Carolus came right out on the landing and listened but he could only hear one side of the conversation—Heatherwell's high-pitched voice raised in surprise, and some excitement, but not in exasperation at having been awakened at this time.

"Oh it's you. Oh, good-evening," he heard Heatherwell say, and after a long pause in which all that was audible was a hoarse suggestion of whispering—"Very kind of you. Thank you. But it's quite all right."

Whisper.

"Oh no, really. Perfectly all right now. Very good of you."

Whisper.

"Did I? Yes, I'm afraid I did. But . . ."

Whisper.

"Oh no. Did I really? How awful. But I'm absolutely all right now."

Whisper. Whisper. Was there a touch of urgency in the sound?

"Thank you. No. No. I'm not alone. Yes. There's someone here."

Whisper.

"Did I say that? It wasn't quite true, so far as this house is concerned. I've got someone staying with me."

Whisper.

"No, I won't. Of course I won't. It was very good of you to come."

Whisper.

"No, I promise I won't. I quite understand. You don't need to worry. I can keep a promise."

Whisper.

"Yes. Sure. Thanks again. Very kind of you."

Brief whisper.

"Good-night."

The front door was closed and bolted again but Heatherwell did not immediately come upstairs. Was he watching from the dining-room windows to see his visitor depart? Or having a drink to recover from the shock of this encounter?

Carolus listened tensely but heard no car being driven away. Then as Heatherwell started slowly climbing the stairs he noiselessly closed his door. He waited till Heatherwell was in his room, then went back to bed.

This time, for several hours there was no sleep for Carolus. What he had overheard seemed to him the first really reliable pointer he had received. Now, like the people of England after each of the early defeats in the second world war, now he knew where he stood. With sudden ease everything fell into place and before he slept he had a solution. It was not cast-iron, it still needed fortifying, but it was a tremendous advance on his previous makeshift theories. The Stabber of Albert

Park, that chimera of the popular press, was no longer a vague shape but a reality with characteristics if not features plainly discernible.

In the morning Heatherwell brought him a cup of tea as usual.

"Someone call last night?" asked Carolus with an affectation of indifference.

Heatherwell hesitated, then said—"Yes. A bore. I had just got to sleep."

"Anything wrong?" yawned Carolus.

"No. It was only young Gates."

"Really? What did he want?"

"I was supposed to be with the Vigilantes last night, that's all. I'd forgotten all about it."

Carolus saw two possible ways of learning the truth. He might flatly accuse Heatherwell of lying and try to scare it from him. Or he might wait till he had seen young Gates and, facing him with proof that it was a lie, work on from there. He believed he knew the identity of the caller but it was essential that he should know it without doubt. For that matter it might conceivably have been young Gates but if so his call had nothing to do with the vigilantes. He decided on the second course and seemed to lose interest in the whole affair.

"I should have thought the vigilantes were growing sick of the job by now," he said stirring his tea. "Looks quite a bright morning," he added.

Heatherwell seemed relieved to find Carolus leaving the subject and offered him another cup of tea.

Because he liked to follow up each point as it occurred he decided to call on Gates as soon as Heatherwell had left. He knew Heatherwell was one of the earliest among the city workers in Crabtree Avenue and with any luck would have gone to the station while Gates was still at breakfast.

In fact he found Gates preparing to leave.

"Really, old man," Gates protested. "This isn't quite the time to call, is it? I'm willing to give any help I can and all that, but eight-forty-five! Are you out for information again? Wait while I get my coat. You'll have to walk down the road with me, I'm afraid. I'm in a rush."

Carolus obediently followed him into the open air.

"Now what is it you want to know? Don't tell me there have been any more phony confessions?"

"Do you remember what time you went to bed last night?"

"Yes. Early. Why?"

"You didn't go out? After, say, ten, I mean?"

"Out? No. Goggins and Tuckman were on duty last night. I had a bit of a cold and my old people insisted that I should go to bed."

"You didn't have to see Heatherwell about anything?"

"Heatherwell? No. What on earth's this about?"

"Just checking up on something. I suppose Goggins and Tuckman would have been together last night?"

"Not necessarily. We've cut down watches now to seven to eleven. It didn't seem worth covering the avenue for any more. All the murders were within those times. So probably Tuckman and Goggins would do two hours each. Say Tuckman from seven to nine and Goggins from nine to eleven. Something like that. Why?"

"And no one would be on duty after eleven?"

"No. We've cut that out."

"You're absolutely sure you didn't call on Heatherwell last night?"

"Absolutely. If you doubt my word you can go back and ask my parents now. My mother came in to see how I was some time after midnight and found me asleep. Why do you ask, though? What happened last night?"

"Nothing, really. Or everything," said Carolus. "Thanks for your information."

He phoned Goggins to hear that it was as Gates thought—Tuckman had taken the earlier watch, Goggins the later. But Goggins had been in bed and asleep before midnight.

Carolus spent the day working on his notes. What last night had revealed seemed even more convincing in the filmy light of day. But he was reduced to infuriating inaction until Heatherwell returned. Had the Detective Superintendent in charge of the case been someone he knew or to whom he could at least give his still circumstantial evidence he would have insisted on an interview. But with Dyke it would be useless.

Heatherwell was due at about 6 o'clock. At 7 he had not appeared. Nor at 8. Nor 9. At 10 o'clock Carolus phoned the landlord of the Mitre and heard that Heatherwell had not been in that evening.

Sixteen

CURIOUS, thought Carolus, how early instincts and obscure rules of conduct persist in ruling our behaviour even in the crises of later life. Here he was at a critical point in one of the most dangerous investigations he had known and he hesitated to examine Heatherwell's papers. It was absurd.

He decided to wait till eleven-thirty and then, if there was no word or sign of Heatherwell, to open the large bureau. After all, other lives might depend on his actions at this point.

In the meantime he phoned Chumside and heard only one small piece of news—of a conversation between two of the men whom Chumside described as on the list—which seemed at all relevant. And occupied as he was in tracing Heatherwell, and learning from him at all costs the identity of last night's caller, Carolus did not connect Chumside's information with his present search.

At eleven-thirty he began to move decisively as though relieved that after all his seeming dilatoriness he could go into action. He swiftly picked the lock of the bureau and found it in a fairly orderly condition. He knew that Heatherwell was a junior partner in a firm of City wine merchants and in a few moments he found some headed notepaper of the firm Nickleby, Roque, Westall and Company. The directors' names were given and he switched to the London Telephone Directory to find that Giles Hatton Westall, the senior partner, lived in Queen's Gate. He dialled his number. In a few moments he heard a lush voice, richly lubricated with port, he felt, enquiring who the devil he was.

Carolus spoke crisply. Heatherwell was missing, he said. He had been due home at six and there was still no word of him.

"Most extraordinary," Westall said. "But young Heatherwell has been behaving rather oddly since his wife left him. Who are you?"

"I'm a friend staying in his house. My name's Deene. Was there anything unusual in his conduct today?"

"He did not return to the office after lunch. That was unusual. He told one of my partners he was not well but said nothing to me."

"Can you account for that?"

"Account for it? I don't know who you are but you've got plenty of impudence. Phoning me at midnight to ask me to account for a man's movements."

"Do you think he might be with his wife?"

"Not if he's in his right mind. She left him. Let him wait for her to come back to him. I've told him so a thousand times."

"It's simply a question of tracing him," said Carolus patiently. "Do you know where she is?"

"I do not and I don't want to know. Women nowadays . . ."

"Yes, yes. But it is essential that I find Heatherwell. Tonight. Now. It may be a matter of life and death."

"Don't talk hysterically. The man must be somewhere. Have you tried the police?"

"No, I have not tried the police. There is every reason not to do so."

"You mean young Heatherwell is in trouble of some kind?"

"He may be. Or someone else may. The thing is, I've got to find him. Can you give me any information that will help me to do so?"

"I have an idea he told me his wife was at Hastings," said Westall less irascibly. "But that was some weeks ago. I can't tell you any more than that. The whole thing is unaccountable to me. What did she want to leave him for?"

Carolus hurriedly said good night and returned the receiver while he looked through the bureau again. It was some minutes before he found two or three letters together. They were in a woman's handwriting and came from the Dukeries Hotel, the Marina, Hastings. One was written only three days ago and all were signed Sarah.

It was his only chance. Hastings was nearly sixty miles away but for once the Bentley's potentialities for speed could be exploited without grave risk. He should be able to reach the Dukeries Hotel before half past one.

His car was in a park in Inverness Road and it took him ten minutes to pull on a coat, reach it and drive off. He knew the way and once he had left the suburbs he could open out. He passed through Sevenoaks at twelve-thirty and Tonbridge ten minutes later, then raced south east towards the coast. It was one-twenty when he came into St. Leonards-on-Sea and a few minutes later pulled up before the fairly large frontage of the Dukeries Hotel.

He had to ring three times before a sleepy night porter blinked at him.

"I thought they was all in," he said sourly.

Carolus briskly and lavishly tipped him.

"I'm not staying in the hotel," he said. "But you have a Mrs. Heatherwell here I think."

"That's right. Number 51."

"Did her husband arrive today?"

"I'm not supposed to say anything about that," said the night porter.

"Has he got the same room?"

The night porter nodded.

"I haven't told you, don't forget."

"It's him I want to see."

"I can't do anything about that except telephone up to the room and say someone's here. What name shall I tell them?"

Carolus hesitated.

"Dyke," he said at last.

The night porter went to the switchboard. After some considerable time he got an answer and said sulkily—

"There's a Mr. Dyke waiting down here."

Another long silence. Then—"All right. I'll tell him." He turned to Carolus. "She's coming down," he said.

"*She's* coming down? But it's Mr. Heatherwell I want to see."

"I'm not supposed to know he's there. It was one of the girls told me. And you don't know either, don't forget. Not from me, you don't."

Presently a handsome young woman with flaming red hair, wearing a shimmering pale green dressing-gown, came down the stairs. It was evident that her husband had told her 'Dyke' was a policeman. She made only a rather feeble attempt to pretend that Heatherwell was not with her.

"What do you want with me?" she asked.

"Nothing, Mrs. Heatherwell. It's your husband I want to see."

"But he's . . ."

"He's upstairs in room number 51. May I see him, please?"

"He's asleep."

"I don't think so. And I haven't come down from London to wait till he wakes up. I'm investigating a triple murder."

"But you can't. He's . . ."

"Yes. I know he doesn't want to see anyone at present. But this is far too urgent a matter to wait till the morning."

Carolus saw that Sarah Heatherwell was dangerously near hysteria. Her hand went up to her face.

"Are you going to arrest him?" she asked.

"No. I only want to ask him a few questions."

"Oh God. What about?"

"One question, really. If he'll answer just one question truthfully it's all I want."

"I *knew* this would happen!"

"Sit down, Mrs. Heatherwell. The night porter will get you a drink."

"The bar's all shut up," said the night porter in his surliest voice.

Carolus nodded to him sharply and he disappeared for a moment to return with a glass.

"Drink that," said Carolus, "while I run upstairs and see your husband. You needn't worry. So long as he tells me one thing."

"It's on the first floor," said the night porter. "Turn to your left at the top of the stairs."

Sarah Heatherwell who had sunk into an armchair began to sob loudly and uncontrollably. Carolus went upstairs.

He found Heatherwell dressed and suspected that he had hurriedly pulled his clothes on when his wife had left him to go downstairs. Yet Heatherwell showed no particular surprise when Carolus entered rather than Dyke.

"Oh, it's you," he said dully. "Are the police downstairs?"

"No. I must apologize for giving Dyke's name. It was absolutely essential that I should see you."

Heatherwell blinked.

"What do you want?" he asked at last.

"Who came to the house last night, Heatherwell?"

"I told you. Gates."

"Gates was in bed. He didn't leave his house last night."

Heatherwell was silent.

"I can't think why you should be so secretive about this."

"I gave my word."

Carolus saw the futility of arguing or trying to make Heatherwell understand his urgency. The man appeared numbed and scarcely aware of his surroundings. He decided to take a chance. He believed that Heatherwell's expression, or some movement, or something in the eyes, would tell him when the name was mentioned and started to ask—"Was it So-and-So? So-and-So?" running through not only Chumside's 'list' but adding three names he had not mentioned to Chumside. Finally, at one, he saw what he expected. Heatherwell tried to control a jerk of his whole body but failed.

"At last," said Carolus and hurried from the room.

In the hall he had time to say—"Your husband's quite all right. But go to him." Then he rushed out to the car, started it, and moved away. He was soon on the London road.

And now it was, what he had so often claimed for issues in his cases, a matter of life and death. That name, combined with what Chumside had told him on the phone three hours ago, meant certainty, and a very ugly certainty at that.

Carolus was unconscious of fatigue. On the contrary he felt something like exhilaration as he sped across Sussex to the Kentish border. He felt justified in ignoring speed limits and barely slowed down for the silent and empty villages. He knew exactly his objective and counted on the powerful engine of his car to enable him to reach it in time.

When he came into the streets of Albert Park it was nearly half past three and the only living being he saw was a policeman on his beat. He drove to the car park from which he had taken his car and left it there. Then he set out for Slatter's lodge at the park gates.

There was no wind or rain tonight, but the air was cold and damp, a dark and somehow miserable night. As he approached the lodge he saw no lights and thought the little stucco house on one floor looked grim and dreary among its close-growing shrubs. He stood outside for a moment listening and looking about him. Of the park behind its iron gates he could see almost nothing but the lodge was built so that its entrance was open to the road.

A porch was over the door and shrubs came close to this on either side. There was no electric bell and no knocker on the door but an iron bell-pull. Carolus heard a cracked sound as his tug at this set a bell ringing within the lodge. This died away bringing no response or movement from within.

Carolus tried again, with the same result. It was a sad sound which seemed to come out of a hollow emptiness as though the lodge had been unoccupied for years. It was hard to believe that within someone was alive, listening perhaps or in deep sleep.

He tried the door handle and found the door opened easily. He pushed it forward a foot and called "Slatter!"

Still no answer.

"Slatter! Are you there?"

Carolus shoved the door wide and stepped into a sitting-room. He groped to a light switch and found it.

The sitting-room was not large and there was too much furniture. A table with a table-cloth nearly filled its space. Carolus caught only a brief impression of this room before crossing to another door, but it was not an impression of a room left by someone retiring to bed. Nothing seemed out of place. The ashtray on the table was empty and clean and the air of the room seemed that of an unoccupied house.

But the house was not, in a sense, unoccupied. Carolus crossed to the door on the far side and flung it open. The light behind him showed someone lying fully dressed on the bed. Again he felt for a switch and illumined the room. The man on the bed was Slatter, lying in a position of complete repose, his eyes shut and his hands lying one on each side of him. He was quite dead.

Having made sure of this Carolus stood contemplating the dead body for nearly a minute. Then his eyes went round the room. There was a bedside lamp and this he had switched on from the door. He crossed to it and saw a switch almost within reach of the dead man's hand. He tried it—a two-way switch. Thoughtfully he returned to the sitting-room and again moved the switches. Here too was a two-way switch, from one doorway to the other. Simple and logical. But both had last been operated by the switch nearest the exit.

He returned to the corpse. Lying beside Slatter on the counterpane was a strong villainous-looking butcher's knife. Over the head of his bed was hung a raincoat, a grey muffler and a cloth cap. On the table by his bedside was a pair of heavy spectacles.

But beside him, too, were several tubes and bottles and one of them, which Carolus recognized, was a soporific, a pheno-barbitone preparation of moderate strength. The bottle was empty and the cap was lying beside it.

"He would have had to take a lot of those to kill himself," thought Carolus and wondered why he had not got hold of one of the pheno-barbitone preparations which contained morphine. Slatter suffered from insomnia and could have obtained the necessary doctor's certificate.

The inference, then, which the first discoverer of this scene was intended to draw was that Slatter was the Stabber and had killed himself by an over-dose of drugs after leaving his weapon and disguise beside him as a confession of his guilt. It was possible, on the known facts, but Carolus did not like it for a number of reasons. It was too neat, too obvious. Then if Slatter wished to confess why didn't he do so unequivocably with pen and paper? And finally, why had he walked over to the front door in the sitting-room to turn *that* light out, and to the door *into* the sitting-room from the bedroom to turn out *this* one?

Carolus returned to the sitting-room and looked about him. His first impression of a room too tidy to have been left by a man going to bed remained. The chairs round the table were set straight, the single grimy cushion in the arm-chair by the range had been patted into place, there wasn't a crumb or a sign of tobacco ash anywhere.

There was another door in the room which led to a small kitchen. Not a dish in the sink, not a used plate on the table. Carolus opened a cupboard and was met by a smell of stale food. 'I always eat a bit of bread and cheese before turning in', he remembered Slatter saying. Yes, here was the cheese, a half ball of yellow Dutch.

Carolus brought it to the light and examined it carefully. It was a little dry and its surface had turned to a deep yellow colour, but from one end of it a piece had been newly cut, showing a pale fresh surface.

He went on to the bread bin. Yes, the loaf too had had a slice cut from it, the surface had not had time to dry.

What then had been Slatter's movements? The two sets of evidence were totally inconsistent. If he had, as it appeared, committed suicide was it credible that he had come home from the Mitre, set out his supper, eaten it, washed up, set everything back in its place, gone to his room after carefully juggling the light switches, and swallowed his whole supply of sleeping tablets, after laying out the articles which constituted his confession? If so, this was the strangest suicide on record.

But suppose he had had no such intention. Suppose he had come home, eaten his supper and then admitted someone. Someone in whose interest it was that he should die. Someone who hearing of his insomnia brought some tablets that would surely give him a good night's rest. Then everything fell into place.

Or again, suppose he had met someone that evening who knew it was his habit not to lock his front door. Someone who suggested he should try *these* tablets to be swallowed an hour before retiring. Someone who could come to the house when they had taken their deadly effect? Once more everything fell into place.

Carolus replaced the cheese and bread and carefully closed the cupboard door. He had entered wearing his motoring gloves and either by intent or guided by instinct he had kept them on. He now switched out the lights leaving the two-way switches as he had found them. Then he stepped out of the lodge quietly shutting the door after him, and walked away.

Seventeen

It was the plain duty of Carolus to go to the nearest police station and report what he had found, or at least to telephone. But here he was up against an awkward predicament. If he reported the matter his name would go into police records as the finder of the body and the press would very soon publish a report of this. He could smile at the headmaster as a good pompous creature, but he took his job seriously and he had promised that his name should not emerge. If he waited till the morning and saw Dyke himself, Dyke would see that it was to his own interest, and to that of the police force, that an efficient policeman should be the first to discover the tragedy and would be willing to leave Carolus out of it.

Nothing much could be lost by keeping his information till the morning, when he could see Dyke personally. So not without misgivings and in full knowledge that he was breaking the law he came quietly and watchfully away from the lodge.

He drove to number 32, this time leaving his car

outside, and within twenty minutes of leaving the lodge he was asleep.

When he had made himself a cup of tea next morning he set out at once for Albert Park Police Station which Dyke had made his headquarters. He still felt no great compunction at not having done this five or six hours earlier but realised that his omission might not endear him to Dyke. Nor would his discovery of the body, for that matter.

He found a spruce sergeant at the desk and asked to see Detective Superintendent Dyke. The sergeant looked at him coolly and asked his name, which Carolus gave. A slip of paper was dispatched by a constable to unknown regions.

"Chilly again this morning," said Carolus to the sergeant who continued to occupy himself with the book in front of him.

A buzzer sounded and the sergeant said, "Yes, sir," several times then turned to Carolus.

"The Superintendent can't see you," he said. "He's too busy. He advises you to get out of Albert Park as soon as possible."

Carolus turned to go.

"That's all right," he said smiling. "You might tell him I came to report a murder, would you?"

"What d'you mean? Are you trying to be funny?" asked the sergeant savagely. "Here! Come back. What do you mean, murder?"

Carolus resisted the temptation to be sarcastic and said, "Just murder, that's all. I happen to have come on the corpse."

The sergeant lost his head a little.

"If you're trying anything on it'll be the worse for you," he told Carolus.

Carolus remained silent.

"I'm not having any larks round here. You said murder."

Disconcertingly, Carolus made no reply.

"If there'd been any murder we'd have heard about it," said the sergeant. "Coming here talking about murder!"

"Well, good morning," said Carolus from the door.

"Wait a minute. If you've got something to report you'd better report it."

"Exactly. That's what I came to do. To Superintendent Dyke."

There was a long pause, then a second slip of paper was dispatched.

Was there something ferocious in the buzz this time?

"He wants to see you, though, sir," said the sergeant unhappily into the telephone. "Yes, that's what he says. I've told him that. Very well, sir."

"He'll see you," said the sergeant shortly. "Take him up will you, Whesker?"

Carolus found Dyke alone behind a desk. They exchanged no greeting.

"What's all this nonsense?" asked Dyke before Carolus could speak.

"Murder," said Carolus.

Dyke watched him craftily.

"Go on, Mr. Deene. Go on. Have your little game. I've warned you once."

"You have indeed. Perhaps I should have let you find the corpse yourself. I expect you would have, some time today."

Dyke made efforts to control himself.

"Whose corpse?" he asked dangerously.

"Slatter's. The park-keeper. He has been poisoned," Carolus replied.

For a moment Dyke hesitated and then the efficient detective that he was got the better of his annoyance.

"Give me full details, please."

"Certainly. That's what I came to do. Slatter is lying, fully dressed, on his bed at the lodge of Albert Park. He died some time during the night, probably from an overdose of sleeping pills. A butcher's knife, presumably the one with which the three earlier murders were committed, is beside him. A raincoat and cap are over the head of his bed. There is also a grey muffler."

"How do you know all this?"

"I happened to call on him, and found what I have described."

"Call on him? What time?"

"Must have been around four o'clock this morning."

Dyke seemed about to break out again but controlled himself.

"What makes you think he was murdered?"

"Ah, there we enter private territory, Superintendent. What makes me think is my own affair. What you will think when you see it all is yours. Let's leave it at that."

"I want to know what took you to Slatter's lodge at four o'clock this morning."

"Shall we say a hunch?"

"You mean you thought you would find what you did?"

"I feared I might. Unfortunately I couldn't get there quicker. I came up from Hastings in less than ninety minutes."

"What's Hastings got to do with it?" asked Dyke despairingly.

"Oh nothing, really. I had to get some information there."

"Mr. Deene," said Dyke at last. "I don't deny I think you're a nuisance. If I had the power to prevent your sort from nosing round I'd do it. It's dangerous in a case like this. And if what you tell me now is true it lays you open to some very serious charges. Very serious. You might even be considered an accessory after the fact."

"Why not the murderer? After all I'm the only person you know of who went to Slatter's lodge last night."

"I've no reason to think yet there has been a murder. All you have told me so far points to suicide."

"You'll soon see for yourself," said Carolus, rising to go.

"You'll be wanted at the Inquest," said Dyke sharply.

"Yes. That's awkward isn't it. I don't want my name in this. Wouldn't it be better for one of your men to 'discover' the corpse? Who is to know that you had prior information? Slatter will be missed at his work by now. What more natural than that a policeman should go to his lodge and find him, then report to you? That, surely, would suit both of us."

Dyke was struggling.

"You'd better be at the Inquest, anyway," he said at last.

Carolus would like to have been present when Sergeant Murdoch, a sturdy member of the uniformed branch, was given instructions to proceed to Albert Park and after obtaining information that Slatter had not appeared that morning go to the lodge to investigate, thereupon telephoning to the Station to state what he had found. Within an hour or less, Carolus calculated, Dyke would be able to make his investigation, the police being solely responsible for the discovery.

All might have been well at the Inquest if Sergeant Murdoch, a dyed-in-the-wool old timer who used every police cliché in the book, had not started to give his evidence with words which had served him well in many a dubious prosecution.

"Acting on instructions," he began. "I proceeded to . . ."

But the Coroner, a lively hawk of a man, was too quick for him.

"Instructions?" he snapped. "What instructions?"

Sergeant Murdoch gaped.

"Instructions to proceed to Albert Park," he replied resentfully without realizing where he was being led.

"*Whose* instructions?" asked the Coroner.

At least Murdoch knew better than to involve the CID man. All his training had taught him to keep his superior officers out of the witness-box.

"The Desk Sergeant said . . ."

"Am I to understand that some information had already been received at the Station?"

Sergeant Murdoch was baffled. Never before had one of his stock phrases been so mauled and shaken in a court.

"Acting on instructions . . ." he tried again.

"I shall require further information on this point," said the Coroner firmly.

So it was that Carolus found himself giving evidence. The Coroner showed him no mercy.

"You are, I understand, a schoolmaster?"

"I am."

"Are you in employment?"

"Yes."

"At what school?"

"The Queen's School, Newminster," admitted Carolus, trying to picture Mr. Gorringer's face when he read his evening paper.

"Are you a resident of Albert Park?"

"I have been staying here during the school holidays."

"Why?"

It was an understandable question in the circumstances. What sane man, it implied, would choose Albert Park for his vacation. But it left Carolus no escape.

"I was interested in the three murders which had taken place here."

"Oh, you were? Interested. You consider yourself, perhaps, a criminologist?"

"I am an abnormally inquisitive person," retorted Carolus calmly.

"Inquisitive about murder?"

"Often, yes."

"Was it inquisitiveness which led you to visit the lodge of Albert Park in the small hours of the morning?"

"Oh yes."

"And what did you expect to find?"

"Rather what I found. At least I feared that."

"Are you calmly telling me that you expected the dead man to take his own life?"

"No. I expected nothing of the sort."

"You are very evasive, Mr. Deene. Please tell me why you went to this lodge as you did?"

"I thought Slatter might be in danger."

"Indeed. If that was so, why didn't you report the matter to the police?"

"It would have been useless. Dyke had made it clear that he wanted no information from me. I had no definite or concrete facts to give him and I have none now. It was guesswork, or instinct, if you like."

"Guesswork told you that Slatter would take his own life?"

"Guesswork told me that Slatter would be murdered."

The Coroner allowed himself a cold stare at Carolus, but did not pursue this point.

"At what time did you find the body?"

"Somewhere round four in the morning."

"At what time did you report it to the police?"

"Five hours later."

"What did you do during those five hours?"

"Slept."

"Knowing a man was lying dead in Albert Park lodge?"

"There was nothing to be done about it."

"Though you believed him to have been murdered?"

"Yes."

"I find your conduct in many respects reprehensible. You appear to have regarded the tragic deaths of three innocent women an occasion for the exercise of your hobby. If you have not impeded the police in the exercise of their duties you have certainly done nothing to assist them. And when you came on the dead body of John Slatter, instead of immediately reporting it you callously went off to bed. It may be that you will have to answer for this in another court and I shall certainly see that the relevant documents are sent to the public prosecutor's office."

A solicitor representing the dead man's family wanted to know what made Carolus think Slatter had been murdered and Carolus referred him to evidence already given that an autopsy had revealed morphine. There was no morphine in tablets of the kind Slatter was presumed to have swallowed. This had already emerged during the hearing of expert evidence and made very little impression now.

The Inquest continued and eventually an open verdict was recorded.

But the evening papers went to town on the Coroner's remarks to Carolus. "Schoolmaster Reprimanded," they halloo'd. "Papers Sent to Public Prosecutor." "Deene Believes Slatter Murdered." " 'Callous' Behaviour of Criminologist."

Carolus decided to escape at once from Albert Park and drove to Crabtree Avenue to collect his belongings from number 32. A group at the gate made him change his mind and he drove on, turning along Cromarty Avenue and down Oaktree Avenue he reached Blackheath and made for Newminster.

Here, he knew, a no less awkward situation awaited him. Mr. Gorringer was a regular reader of the evening papers and although none of them had actually mentioned the school's name he would regard this as 'smirched' by the inclusion, in a most unfavourable light, of his history master. Then Mrs. Stick, who had so often threatened to leave Carolus when he had become involved in what she called his nasty cases, might really make good her threats. Her sister in Battersea, respectably married to someone 'in the Undertaking', whose disapproval Mrs. Stick feared above everything, might already have read and telephoned. Altogether it was an unhappy prospect.

But Carolus was less seriously depressed by this, than by the belief that he had failed to prevent the death of Slatter and that even now he was leaving Albert Park with his hard-gained theory about all these murders unrevealed. If he was right, he was leaving a murderer free, and one who had proved that he would stop at nothing.

Moreover he was leaving the people in the suburb

behind him further disquieted. Several of them had trusted him with information and assistance in order that he might relieve their anxieties by identifying the murderer. Miss Cratchley, with whom he had talked on the phone, was bitterly disappointed in him. The relatives and friends of the dead women had seemed to have confidence in him and in some sense he had failed them.

His best hope was to formulate his case and somehow persuade the police to consider it, if they had not already come to similar conclusions. Only if they would do this could the matter be cleared up. He had not the power or the facilities for following the various clues which were in their hands—he was, he felt wretchedly, no more than a theoritician while they looked for hard proof. The raincoat, the knife, the cloth cap, the muffler and the spectacles, these were what could hang someone or send him to Broadmoor. Carolus could only suggest a line of enquiry. But he believed he was right and determined to set out his case as convincingly as possible. After that, it would be up to Dyke.

He was putting the car in the garage at Newminster when he saw his least favourite pupil awaiting him.

"Oh dear, oh dear, sir, you've done it now," said Priggley. " 'Schoolmaster Reprimanded'. I suppose it had to come. But you've certainly raised hell this time."

"Take yourself off, will you?"

"You see what comes of sending me away? You're simply not to be trusted with a murder, sir. I suppose while this character Slatter was being poisoned you were off on one of your wild chases in that rattler of yours. Collecting vital evidence, or something equally corny."

Carolus walked past him but Priggley followed.

"You simply can't go on like this, you know. It's too

late for you now to be one of those steely-nerved, hard-faced tough boys who face danger every time they go near a case and leap about like crickets among the corpses. You can't do Raymond Chandler stuff. But what about Maigret? Your whole style's lacking in finish, sir. All you do is interview the dullest people and absorb the atmosphere, or something. It's too much."

Carolus was nearly home.

"Oh, I've no doubt you know who the murderer is. You'll pull that name out of the bag all right. I give you that. But it's not enough, sir. We want surprises, escapes, dangers all along the line."

"Who are 'we'?"

"I should have said your fans until a short time ago. But they're falling off. You've disappointed them. The most you ever achieve in the way of sensation is a comfortably fast run in a car."

Carolus prepared to enter his home and close the front door on this odious boy.

"Anyway you've had it this time. Gorringer's blowing his top. As for Mrs. Stick—you wait till you see Mrs. Stick. Even my merry humour couldn't draw a smile from her. She has got to Speak, she says. She has let it go too long. She might have known it would come to this. She was only saying to Stick. One way and another, sir, you're in for a very difficult day or two. Perhaps you had forgotten that the summer term, so called, starts tomorrow? Your colleagues will welcome you to the common-room, no doubt, after seeing that you have been publicly reprimanded. 'Papers Sent to Public Prosecutor'. Gorringer will love that. But sir, why didn't you keep me with you?"

"I ought to have. You might have been murdered."

"I could have saved you from the wildest of your

gaffes. Why on earth didn't you report the thing when you found it? You had only to go to a telephone."

"That didn't matter. What matters is that the murderer is still at large."

" 'At large'. How Valentine Vox can you get? And which murderer, anyway?"

"There's only one," said Carolus as though to himself.

"And you know him?"

"I know who it is."

"Can you prove it?"

"No, but the police could."

"Can you persuade them to?"

"I'm going to try."

"Oh God! One of those interminable statements of yours, full of deduction and elegant phraseology. Why can't you catch one murderer at least on the job. Or chase him through the slums of Manchester or something? You need *action* to re-establish what reputation you once had."

"It's not my line, I'm afraid, Priggley. Now run along, will you?"

"You'd better let me come in and face Mrs. Stick with you. I have more influence with her than you."

"Oh very well," said Carolus wearily and entered his house.

Eighteen

MRS. STICK ominously said nothing while she brought in the decanter and siphon and set them beside Carolus. There was perhaps a hostile flash in her steel-rimmed glasses and her thin lips were compressed to a faint pink line. At first it seemed that she would leave the room with her store of outrage, but at the door she turned.

"It's no good, sir. I shall have to Speak. I've seen what it says in the papers, and there's nothing for it but to give you a month's notice for me and Stick."

"I'm sorry to hear that, Mrs. Stick. I thought you were both quite happy here."

"So we was until you started larking about with murderers until we never knew from one day to another if you'd get your throat cut or what raggle-raggle would be coming to the house."

"Do you mean me, Mrs. Stick?" asked Priggley innocently.

Mrs. Stick never took her eyes from Carolus and answered as though he had asked the question.

"No, sir, I don't mean the young gentleman as you very well know. Though what his father and mother would say to see him traipsing round after murderers I don't know. I mean policemen and poisoners and I don't know what ruffians who say they want to give you information so that my heart jumps into my mouth every time I hear a ring at the door. It's not to be borne, it isn't really and I said to Stick today, we shall have to Go, I said."

"You can't do that, Mrs. Stick," said Rupert Priggley. "Who's going to make a game pie for us like you do?"

"That I don't know. Though I say it, there's not many can turn out a patty der jib yer like I can, but you ought to have thought about that before. Now with the Judge telling you he's going to send you to prison . . ."

"Coroner, Mrs. Stick, and his threat was quite empty."

"That's not what the papers say and your picture all over the *Evening Sentinel*. What my sister's going to think I don't know, married as she is to a most respectable party in the Undertaking."

"I should have thought she was accustomed to mortality," said Carolus, making a retort he had longed for years to pronounce.

"That's as may be," said Mrs. Stick darkly. "But think of the Disgrace! It's bad enough your being mixed up in all those horrors without you being stood up in court and reprimanded and I don't know what. What the headmaster's going to say I can't bear to think. He's not going to let you go on teaching young boys like that if they send you to prison."

"It would be difficult," admitted Carolus. "But I think you're taking rather a gloomy view, Mrs. Stick. These things soon blow over."

"Not with me, they don't. I was only saying to Stick, this is the end, I said. We can't go on working for a gentleman who's liable to be arrested any minute and even if he's not is disgraced in the papers. Flesh and blood won't stand it, sir."

Was that a tear behind the flashing spectacles?

"Well, Mrs. Stick, you must do as you think right."

"It's not so much that," admitted Mrs. Stick. "It's all the Talk. I don't hardly dare put my head out of the door with what they're saying. As for Stick . . ."

"Yes, what about Stick?" asked Carolus who secretly believed he had an ally, if not a very powerful one, in Stick.

"He doesn't like leaving his garden after he's made it what it is, but there you are. I told him the other day, how d'you know you're not going to find a corpse when you're digging out there one of these fine days, I asked him. There's corpses enough in all conscience. It's a shame for him to have to give it up when he's so proud of it, but this time there's no two ways about it. Not after you being had up in court for interfering, sir. So I must ask you to take a month's notice and that's it."

There was a break in her voice in the last sentence and she closed the door silently behind her.

But the greatest ordeal for Carolus came next day when the Queen's School, Newminster, had assembled for the new term. At first it was difficult to predict just what the attitude of Mr. Gorringer, the headmaster, might be. He accepted the cheerful greeting of Carolus after morning prayers with a silent and severe inclination of his head. Two periods of teaching were safely negotiated and the eleven o'clock Break had begun before there was any demonstration.

Carolus was the first in the Common-Room and

seized the *Times* crossword with avidity before Hollingbourne could ravish its virginity by the dubious solution of two clues. But when the rest of the staff had gathered there was an unprecedented interruption. The school porter appeared.

Muggeridge was a disgruntled individual who for many years had resented the headmaster's orders that he should wear a uniform consisting of a frock coat and gold-braided top-hat.

"These niceties of appearance," Mr. Gorringer explained, "help to keep a certain dignity for this ancient foundation."

"There's not much dignity when my topper goes for a Burton," grumbled Muggeridge.

But the uniform remained and now appeared in the doorway of the Common-Room.

"He wants you," said Muggeridge. The three words were adequate. The headmaster wanted Carolus.

"Don't ask me what for," went on Muggeridge. "He's got one of his high and mighty fits on. I could tell as soon as I heard the way he rang that blasted bell. I was just having my tea when it started."

Carolus regretfully abandoned his crossword which was taken up by Hollingbourne.

Muggeridge's tale continued as he followed Carolus down the passage.

"I found him sitting up there like a heathen idol. 'I want to speak to Mr. Deene', he says. 'Well can't you speak to him,' I asked him, 'without me running about all the morning? I was just having my tea,' I said. He puts on his grand manner and says 'Kindly summon Mr. Deene, Muggeridge, and make no further comment'. So there you are. *I* don't know."

It was obvious to Carolus, too, that the headmaster

was enjoying one of his 'high and mighty fits'. He was writing at his large desk when Carolus entered and beyond indicating a chair with the end of his fountain pen, showed no sign of awareness of Carolus's arrival. There was a long silence broken by Mr. Gorringer clearing his throat with a mighty rumble. At last he put down his pen and looked up.

"Now, Deene," he said, and paused again.

"What I am about to say to you is in the highest degree painful to me. For many years now we have been colleagues, and, so far as it is allowable between a headmaster and one of his senior assistants, friends. I have never belittled, nay, I have frequently applauded, your unique abilities as a teacher of history, and I do so again. But I should be failing in my duty to the Governors of the Queen's School, to the parents who entrust their sons to our care, to the old boys, to the staff and not least to our pupils if I did not—with the deepest regret, mark you—ask you to resign your post here."

"Certainly, headmaster. On what grounds?"

"Grounds, Mr. Deene? In the circumstances I should scarcely have thought you would wish me to particularise. Let the words of the Coroner be sufficient. I have nothing to add to them. That an assistant of mine should have laid himself open to public reprimand in a matter so alien to his rightful profession, that he should actually be threatened with prosecution over his conduct is . . . seems to me . . . I am sorry. I find it too painful to talk about. I am outraged, Mr. Deene. I can use no other word."

"Yes. I see you are. But don't you think the relatives of the three murdered women feel outraged too, headmaster?"

"The feelings of these unfortunate people, much though I sympathize with them, are no possible concern of ours in this quiet backwater of learning. And may I ask what you have done to relieve them? As I understand the matter the identity of their murderer is not yet entirely removed from the realms of speculation."

"That's so."

"Had you gone quietly to this unhappy suburb and by dint of your undoubted though misdirected talents been of some assistance to the police investigating, had you as in other cases, anonymously indicated a possible solution to a difficult problem, I might have found some answer to the Governors. I might have assisted you to ride the storm of opprobrium which you have raised. But you have not done so."

"I know who is the murderer, if that's what you mean," said Carolus quietly.

For a moment Mr. Gorringer pretended to ignore this, though his great red ears with their hairy orifices, almost flapped as he heard the words.

"You know, Deene," he said, relaxing a little. "How very painful all this is to me. You say you *know* who is the guilty party?"

"Yes."

"In all three of these . . . hm . . . assassinations?"

"In all four."

"It is actually the same man—or woman?"

"It is."

"Have you given this information to the authorities?"

"Not yet. I can't prove my case. The police will have to do that."

"But you *have* a case, Deene?"

"Oh, certainly."

"And you intend to state it?"

"If I can get Dyke, the Detective Superintendent investigating, to listen."

"I see. It does not unhappily alter the position vis-a-vis the Governors of this school, but it relieves my private feelings somewhat. I have told you before, Deene, that under this academic gown there beats a very human heart, and it was partly the feeling that you had failed in this case which disturbed me. I cannot yet withdraw my request for your resignation. That, alas, is out of my hands. Sir Boxley Withers, our most respected Chairman, was on the telephone to me this morning."

"What did he want?"

"I am bound to say he was temperate, most temperate, in his disapproval. He even showed a certain levity in his approach. But I can read between the lines and it has come to my ears that others of the Board feel strongly. If events should conspire to justify your conduct, Deene, it might be possible to persuade the Board to take a more lenient view. But for the moment I must insist on your resignation."

"I'll send it you in writing," said Carolus cheerfully.

"In the meantime, if as I suspect you intend to formulate your arguments, to state your case, as it were, I will take the bold step of asking Sir Boxley to be present. It might—who knows?—soften the blow this has been to him, and all of us."

"I don't mind old Withers being there. He's not without intelligence. But the man I have to get is Dyke."

"And when, may I ask, do you intend to expatiate?"

"I need some days to work on my notes."

"I appreciate that. I must remind you, too, that another term has begun and we must not neglect our pedagogic duties," said Mr. Gorringer blandly.

"Say next Wednesday? If you and Withers would care to dine?"

"I shall have to consult Sir Boxley on his engagements. For my own part I am fortunately free on that evening."

"I shall feel like Scheherazade," said Carolus. "Yarning to avert the ax."

Mr. Gorringer did not permit himself to smile.

"I think my ears caught the sound of the school bell," he said severely. "Our third period has begun."

On returning to his house at lunch-time Carolus found his troubles multiplying.

"They've been coming here all the morning," stated Mrs. Stick crisply. "Nor they won't take no for an answer though I threatened to call the police if this went on. One of them went so far as to put his foot in the door."

"Who has been annoying you, Mrs. Stick?"

"Reporters, they said they was. I've scarcely had time to turn round and lunch won't be ready till I don't know when. I wonder they haven't broken into the school after you."

"As they haven't I don't think you need worry any more. It's nearly twenty-four hours since the Inquest so I'm quite passé as news. These must have been strays."

"Whatever they was they upset my cooking. I was going to do you a *sole mew nair*."

"Do by all means, Mrs. Stick," said Carolus abstractedly.

Somehow he had to persuade Dyke to listen to him. It was the only hope of clearing his own conscience and winding up this whole lamentable case. He had certain information which the police had not, but it was of a kind, in itself, that would make very little appeal to them. If he merely catalogued this and handed it over, Dyke would probably ignore it and think him impertinent and interfering. He had to go farther and persuade Dyke to hear what conclusions he had drawn from it.

Perhaps it would be best to return once more to Albert Park and take the bull by the horns. Dyke had had his pound of flesh and heard the Coroner's scathing remarks to Carolus. He might relent sufficiently to listen to him. After all, in what Carolus guessed to be Dyke's point of view, even the murder or suicide of Slatter was irrelevant to the main problem and the continuing danger. A maniacal killer had stabbed three women and was still unidentified. Jack the Ripper, who provided the only known precedent in English criminal history for a series of murders of this kind, had twice waited five months or more between two of his murders and there seemed no reason why the Stabber should not do the same. Could Dyke afford to ignore someone who claimed he had a theory to identify him?

After school that afternoon Carolus drove back to Albert Park and was relieved to find that Dyke agreed to see him at once.

"You see what comes of meddling, Mr. Deene?" the Superintendent greeted him.

"I see what comes of *not* meddling. All I wanted was that the police should seemingly make that discovery for themselves. That's why I waited for the morning to see you. However, I shan't lose any sleep over the Coroner's remarks."

"What do you want to see me about this time? Found any more corpses?"

"Not yet. I came to invite you to dinner on Wednesday."

Dyke stared at him.

"Now what's this?" he said. "You ought to know by now that if there's one thing I hate it is a practical joke."

"So do I. Detest them," said Carolus. "I'll be perfectly frank, Superintendent. I have got a theory in this wretched business which I very much want you to consider. I understand that in your official capacity you cannot listen to the lucubrations of amateur detectives, but as a private individual after a dinner party you could surely do so."

"I could, if I thought it would help me. Are you suggesting that you have identified this Stabber?"

"Provisionally, yes."

"What do you mean by provisionally, Mr. Deene?"

"Unless I can persuade you to consider my theory at least as a possibility it will die stillborn. I have not a scrap of proof—only a lot of circumstantial evidence. But if I am right the hard proof is there for you and your forensic experts to uncover."

Dyke smiled.

"You speak as though I had formed no opinions of my own," he said. "All right, Mr. Deene. I accept your invitation and am grateful for it."

Carolus arranged to come over in the car and pick him up.

Back once again in Newminster he was amazed to find a faint smile on the lips of Mrs. Stick.

"I've had a letter from my sister, sir," she said almost amicably. "I was never more surprised in my life. She says her husband says you were quite right and it was a wicked thing for that Coroner to start on you like that, when all you was doing was your duty as a citizen. You could have bowled me over when I read it. You never can tell with people, can you, sir?"

"Indeed you can't, Mrs. Stick."

"So all things considered and Stick not liking to give up his garden, I thought . . ."

"Just so. I quite understand and am delighted. Now I want to give a small dinner-party on Wednesday. Only six of us, a stag party. Can you manage that?"

A shadow of repressed doubt crossed Mrs. Stick's face.

"Well," she began.

"The headmaster and one of the school Governors, Sir Boxley Withers, will be among them," said Carolus hurriedly.

"Then I must see what I can do. We could start with a nice *print an year* soup . . ."

Carolus left Mrs. Stick happily planning her menu.

Nineteen

At dinner on the following Wednesday Mr. Gorringer was jovial. It was impossible for him to be in any gathering without in some sense taking the chair and in spite of the presence of Sir Boxley Withers he did so now.

"Ah Deene," he congratulated. "Your enviable Mrs. Stick is excelling herself. She is indeed a treasure. When I told my wife that I was dining here tonight she made one of her happier witticisms. 'Screw your courage to the sticking-place', she said. I must say I laughed heartily."

There was a somewhat puzzled look on the puckered face of Withers, a small neat man in his sixties. He was not the first to be perplexed by Mr. Gorringer's humour. Dyke, though he said little, seemed perfectly at home. Priggley was of course irrepressible.

"You may well wonder," Mr. Gorringer said later in private to Withers, "that I should lend my presence to a gathering of this kind when one of my pupils has been invited. But this, Sir Boxley, is a somewhat unusual case. Unfortunate home life. Lack of parental control. Deene assures me that if he did not exercise some influence in the holidays, this boy would be completely unbridled. So I find it wise to disregard the impropriety of allowing a boy to dine at the same table as his headmaster."

Again Withers gave him his incredulous stare as though wondering whether Gorringer could possibly be true.

Priggley brought over a box of cigars.

"No, don't take those," he advised the headmaster. "They're on the dry side. I recommend the Ramon Allones." He turned to Withers. "Brandy, sir?" he suggested. "Carolus has got some very decent Otard VVSOP, or there's some Armagnac which I find just a shade too old."

"Priggley," said Mr. Gorringer severely. "I don't think Sir Boxley wishes to be lectured on the comparative merits of brandies."

"I'll have the Otard," put in Withers.

"You see what I mean?" said Mr. Gorringer when Priggley had left them. "The boy is sadly out of hand."

"He was quite right about the cigars," was all that Withers said.

Presently there was a general move towards comfortable chairs and an atmosphere of expectancy began to grow. Lance Thomas, the school doctor and an intimate friend of Carolus, made the sixth, and seemed as interested as everyone else, though he knew no more of the case than newspaper readers all over the country.

When Carolus began talking it was quietly, almost casually.

"More than once in this case the name of Jack the

Ripper has turned up and in a way it is the key to the whole thing. There can't be many people alive today who can remember the fear and horror which passed over the East End of London in the years 1888 to 1889 when no less than ten women, all prostitutes, were murdered by a killer who remained, and has since remained, unidentified. The case has tempted several criminologists to speculate but nothing is known certainly except that all the women were killed by one blood-lustful man. I say this is the key to the present case because I believe that the Stabber we have to find deliberately imitated the Ripper of history.

"When I started to enquire into this I found myself believing, as everyone else did, that a homicidal maniac was at work. I do not like believing what everyone else does and began asking myself why I did so. Because these were obviously the murders of a homicidal maniac. Because anything else would be too horrible to contemplate. But I distrust the obvious and nothing, in human nature, is too horrible to contemplate.

"By this way I began to make suppositions. Suppose these were not the murders of a maniac but the very carefully planned murders of someone with a logical motive. Motive? How could anyone have a motive for killing each one of these three women? A madman's motive there might be, to kill all women, or to kill all small women, or to kill all the women in Albert Park. But I was looking for saner motives than these.

"You see, I don't like the literary idea of a schizophrenic. I absolutely reject *Dr. Jekyll and Mr. Hyde.* I believe in a split mind but not in dual personality. Certainly each side of a split mind will influence the other. It is impossible to have two souls inhabiting one body and taking over the controls in turn. So if my murderer was sane and had a motive it was a consistent one.

"This led me to a line of speculation which at first rather appalled me. Since there could only be a sane motive in *one* of these cases, were the others motiveless? Or were two victims chosen haphazardly to conceal one victim for whose death there was a very distinct motive?

"I began then to suppose that someone wanted to kill one of these three women and, of course, to remain undetected. He decides to create a mysterious killer, a Jack the Ripper, a Stabber, who kills without purpose any woman he sees at night in the Albert Park region. The more publicity this receives the better. It will divert all the attention from him or her, the person with a motive for one murder, to the Stabber, an insane killer who has no motive at all.

"But even if I accepted this idea it did not tell me which of the three murders was, as it were, the real one. The killer might make it his first murder and cover it by the subsequent ones. Or he might sandwich the murder he wanted to commit between two done to mislead. Or he might make the 'real' murder the third of three.

"My supposition, gruesome though it was, began to take possession of me, and as most people formed some sort of image of the Stabber, (so that Viola Whitehill really believed she had seen his glaring eyes,) so I formed a conception of the killer.

"I could not decide whether he was a resident of Albert Park; he certainly knew the suburb well and the movements of the residents. Only one of the three women actually lived in the district but the other two visited it, one at weekly and the other at daily intervals. He might himself live in Crabtree Avenue or he might be someone who had lived in the suburb and had moved away. Or someone with copious information. Or a regular visitor.

"He created a physical image of the killer by adopting a costume which could be changed in a moment, which had no element of the exotic, yet which was enough to distinguish him—the raincoat, cloth cap, and glasses which Miss Pilkin observed before the third murder. The raincoat was a little too large for him because he did not wear his own and had probably acquired the other by theft, just as warehouse breakers always use a stolen car for their getaway. In fact, the first piece of evidence which might be acquired by the police, who have the facilities, is news of a raincoat lost in some public place in the last months . . ."

Dyke, though determined not to be drawn, could not resist this.

"We've been working on that for days and have reduced our number down to a hundred and thirty-seven. In due course we shall know who was the original owner of the raincoat found in the lodge and perhaps know how he lost it."

"Of course," said Carolus. "You would not miss that. Indeed I have believed all along that that raincoat and the cap, glasses, muffler and knife will convict. However to return to my supposititious murderer.

"On the night he has chosen he waits among the trees at the top of Crabtree Avenue for the last woman or girl to emerge alone from the school. That is, unless Hester Starkey is his 'real' victim. At a propitious moment, when no one is in sight, Hester comes out and starts walking down the avenue towards the more brilliantly lighted Inverness Road at its foot. She walks firmly and fairly fast, but with long strides he keeps behind her till she passes Perth Avenue and reaches number 46, the empty house. Here, with a skilled downward blow between the shoulder blades he strikes and in almost complete silence Hester collapses and dies. He picks up the body, puts it in the garden of the empty house, and . . .

"But this is the interesting thing. He does not go home, wherever that is. He has been exhilarated by his grim success and feels a sudden reaction to it. He wants to be among other people. He takes off his raincoat, cap and glasses and with them leaves his identity as the Stabber. But before he can go among people he must make sure that he carries no blood stains. So he goes, logically enough, to the public convenience at the foot of Salisbury Gardens and calmly has a wash and brush up. The lavatory attendant described his behaviour. 'You should have seen the way he washed. Taking his time over it. Then when he's not washing any more he's standing looking at himself in the glass . . . this way that way, looking at his sleeves and his trousers.' He has no idea that he has attracted the attention of the attendant, or that use of a wash-basin at this time of the evening is a not very common occurrence. He thinks he is one of an uncounted string of men using the lavatory. He comes out, and unless I am mistaken goes along to the Mitre. He thus picks up the threads of his normal life without the slightest suspicion attaching to him.

"The second murder is even easier. With each of these we are assuming, illogically, that it is not the 'real' one, not the one the murderer had in mind from the start. In this case, though it sounds a callous expression to use, the murderer had practice. He carries it out with more confidence and once again goes to the public convenience afterwards to wash.

"But when he comes to the third he is faced with

various problems. He exists now, the Stabber has become a real person in the minds of many frightened people. Crabtree Avenue is being watched by the police and householders. It is essential that he shows this murder to have been done by the same hand as the others so he decides to keep to Albert Park while moving to another street. He is fortunate in having in Salisbury Gardens another gloomy, ill-lit residential street on the far side of the park, but this time there is a very keen observer of a certain portion of the street at least for the eccentric Miss Pilkin allows nothing to escape her in her malicious watch on the Pressley household. From what she sees the Stabber emerges as a man in a raincoat a little too large for him, with a cloth cap and glasses. But this does nothing to identify him for even if Miss Pilkin knew the man concerned, this simple disguise would be enough to confuse her.

"This time he does not go down to the public convenience or to the Mitre. But he has achieved his third murder without being caught in the only way he believes it is possible to be caught, that is in the very act. Three women have been killed by an unknown Stabber and among them is the woman he meant to kill.

"Mad? Oh yes. In a certain sense raving mad. It would take a madman, fortunately, to be so far beyond all scruple, all respect for human life, all morality, that he could conceive such a plan. Yet there was a macabre logic in this madness. If one is prepared to arrogate to oneself the power of God to take *one* life, why not *three?* It is no more presumptuous. The appalling thing is that one human being can contemplate the killing of another.

"At this point, I believe, he was prepared to stop, not because he had any scruple about killing again if it was necessary but simply because it wasn't necessary. There would be no point in it. He had all England and the CID looking for a maniacal homicide who had slain three women in the same way and in the same suburb. No one suspected him. His achievement was complete.

"If he had stopped there I do not think he would ever have been discovered, but like Jack the Ripper before him have remained a teasing mystery for criminologists thereafter. But he could not stop there. Perhaps he feared that he might be discovered. Or perhaps he was one of those people—and how many there are—who cannot leave their achievements alone, who have to embellish and add till they ruin their own handiwork.

"At all events he decided to divert all suspicion from himself by arranging a suicide. Someone who could have been responsible for all three murders must die, leaving what appeared to be a confession of his guilt beside him in the shape of the raincoat, which would have traces of bloodstains however it had been cleaned at home, the cap, the glasses, the muffler and the knife, none of which for one reason or another could be connected with the real murderer, though all would be assumed to have belonged to the Stabber.

"This was a clumsy idea which went beyond the original probably long-contemplated plan. Intended to crown this, it in fact undermined it. At first the murderer seemed fortunate for he discovered that a man called Heatherwell, something of a psychotic, was living alone in Crabtree Avenue and had been alone since his wife left him before the first murder. He met him on several occasions in the Mitre and I think acquired a certain ascendancy over him. He may also have discovered that Heatherwell was a transvestist which would make his guilt and suicide more credible. He planned to kill Heatherwell by using Heatherwell's trust in him to administer an overdose of sleeping pills. He actually came to the house with this purpose but to his alarm heard from Heatherwell that he was not alone, for I had taken the precaution of becoming his guest. When he heard at the door that Heatherwell had someone in the house he hastily obtained a promise from Heatherwell that his visit should not be revealed and disappeared. Heatherwell was a man who kept his promises, or perhaps feared the murderer for the reason I have suggested. Heatherwell preferred to tell me a foolish lie rather than state who had called on him. If he had not done this and thereupon rushed down to Hastings to join his wife, I should have insisted on seeing Dyke at this point, telling him my suspicions and perhaps have saved Slatter's life.

"As it was, I arrived too late, though with the knowledge I now had I was able to follow the movements of both Slatter and the murderer pretty well. They had been talking together for some time at the Mitre as I had heard from Chumside. Slatter, I knew, suffered from insomnia which gave the murderer a splendid opening. He accompanied him to his lodge, perhaps shared his supper of bread and cheese or perhaps watched him eat it, then on the pretext of giving him something that really *would* cure his sleeplessness he gave him his overdose. When Slatter began to feel the effects he told him to lie on his bed for a moment and Slatter fell into the sleep from which he could not wake.

"I find the thought of the next hour or two more spine-chilling than anything connected with the earlier murders. Our man had to wait in the house till he was sure that Slatter was beyond revival, a considerable time in fact. When I reached the lodge between half past three and four I had the feeling—no more than that—that he had not been gone long. Moreover he had to set in position the articles of his disguise and the knife. And since a man about to commit suicide would seem unlikely to have consumed a hearty supper of bread and cheese he had removed all signs of a meal having been eaten.

"He made two mistakes that I noticed, but probably many more have already been discovered by the police. He left the bread and the cheese in their receptacles, each showing that recent cuts had been made from them. And he left the two-way light switches turned off from the wrong ends.

"The Coroner's Inquest, as we know, did not accept the position as the murderer hoped. In the state of psychotic exaltation induced by the successful murder of the three women, he felt he could do no wrong. He was sure that it would never be doubted that Slatter was the Stabber and that Slatter had killed himself. But in this he failed for the verdict was an open one."

Mr. Gorringer raised his hand.

"There, my dear Deene, let us pause and consider. Your brilliant exposition has us all enthralled. Eh, Superintendent?"

Dyke said nothing and Withers still stared in wonder at the headmaster.

"At all events you must not exhaust yourself before reaching what must surely be the climax of your story. Pause, my dear fellow, and refresh yourself."

"Yes. Let's have a drink," said Carolus.

"Fair enough," agreed Priggley and busied himself with the bottles.

"What dark regions there are in the human mind," reflected Mr. Gorringer weightily. "What jungles, and what slums may flourish in those grey cells. For my part

I cannot see why you hesitate to call this unnamed assassin insane. That he may, as you say, have had a cogent motive in one of these murders, does nothing to convince me. I see here the work of a dangerous lunatic. What say you, Sir Boxley?"

It seemed that Withers was startled from his wrapt contemplation of the headmaster. He hesitated then started slightly and said, "Yes. Yes."

"I am glad to find Sir Boxley agrees with my prognosis. This is a most tragic affair."

"What I don't understand," said Rupert Priggley to Carolus, "is why you are bending over backwards not to name the murderer. You obviously know, or think you know, who done it. So why be coy, sir? Why not let us have it and be done with it?"

Carolus, like Withers, seemed to awaken.

"Name the murderer?" he said. "Why not? It was, of course, Jim Crabbett."

Twenty

"'Of course'!" bellowed Mr. Gorringer. "I like your 'of course', Deene. To me it would seem that you had merely picked haphazardly among the possible candidates, and I daresay others of your interested audience feel the same. Why 'of course'?"

" 'The why is plain as way to parish church,' " said Carolus, "and I thought you must all have seen it from the time I began talking about supposition. We supposed a man with a motive for killing one of these three women, and who in the world had such a thing except the husband of that rich, pretentious, domineering woman Hermione d'Avernon Crabbett?

"I reached this to some extent by a process of eliminating the other two. I found that Hester Starkey had inspired rather intense emotions among the staff at St. Olave's Ladies College, but neither Grace Buller, the hefty and sentimental games mistress, nor Gerda Munshall, the somewhat excessive 'great friend' of Hester, could possibly qualify or name anyone else who might do so. Eamon Starkey was eliminated by complete lack of motive, but inquiries and timing, in spite of his phony alibi, would have shown a practical impossibility in his case.

"So Hester Starkey was out. We are apt to think motives for murder are common. 'I could have killed her', we hear people say. But in reality it is not difficult to discover whether anyone could have a motive for killing anyone else, and I was soon convinced that no one known to Hester Starkey wanted her dead, though some of her pupils may have thought they did.

"It was the same when I came to Joyce Ribbing. I met her husband, her sister, her lover and several of her friends in Albert Park. They were rather stuffy people, for the most part, and seemed to have recovered from the shock of Joyce's death very quickly, but among them there was not a suggestion of motive. Both husband and lover had obviously been through great distress at their loss. Here again I could not *feel* anything to awaken suspicions. And as the whole thing so far was working on suspicion and supposition I dismissed the murder of Joyce Ribbing from my mind.

"But when I came to the third murder there was an immediate change of atmosphere and I found some open hatred. Miss Pilkin hated the Pressleys and they hated her. Pressley had quarrelled with his father-in-law and Miss Pilkin had known 'angry disputes between Harry Pressley and Mrs. Crabbett'. 'Pressley seemed to be threatening his mother-in-law with violence'. 'There were other disputes, sometimes between Pressley and his wife'. And so on.

"But it was when I went out to Bromley to see Jim Crabbett that my suspicions began to coalesce. It was pretty obvious that Crabbett had for years detested his wife's social pretentiousness. 'She liked to be addressed as d'Avernon Crabbett' he said and added unnecessarily and significantly, 'Harmless, really. I didn't mind'. He went on to speak of her 'kind nature' and the local charities she supported with a sort of concealed bitterness which I did not like. Mrs. Crabbett was wealthy; Crabbett had nothing and even his job he had had to give up. 'There was no need for me to continue and my wife . . . we liked to be together'. Later when I suggested that his wife might have waited for him at her daughter's that evening, another flash came out involuntarily. 'You didn't know her', Crabbett said, then amended this with, 'She was so punctual herself always'.

"A picture emerged of a weak man, secretly resentful, being the lackey of his rich wife and having no way of re-establishing his lost independence until or unless he inherited her money. That after her death he immediately began to do the things he had long wanted to do was apparent to me during my visit to Bromley. I guessed he had banished all photographs of his wife from the living-room when he fetched one whose frame matched those remaining there, but this was only a guess. More significant was his acquisition, 'only a few days' before I saw him of a puppy whose 'family' he had known for a long time. It was not fanciful to picture him wanting one of a friendly dog's litter and knowing that Mrs. d'Avernon Crabbett would never stand for a mongrel, or a dog at all for that matter. 'She couldn't bear dogs', her daughter said. Jim Crabbett had lost no time after her death.

"Then there was the well-stocked drink cabinet which he had 'found in a furniture shop yesterday' and from which he proudly offered me a drink as, perhaps, he had longed to offer one many times during his wife's teetotal regime. In this too he was enjoying his emancipation.

"But he had not enjoyed his last years with Hermione. 'I'm sorry for him, really,' said his daughter. 'He does not seem to take an interest in anything'. 'It's not very nice to talk about it, but it was mother who had the money. Dad retired ages ago, without much of a pension . . . Mother wanted him to.' And he, who as he told me could do anything in a house 'from cooking to turning out a room' found himself completely under his wife's domination.

"Yes. He was the only one with a motive. But that was no more than the beginning of my circumstantial trail. Hester Starkey was murdered on Thursday February 8th, Joyce Ribbing on the 22nd and Hermione Crabbett on March 15th. The Press made something of this clockwork regularity but did not notice the full force of it. It was on Thursdays that Crabbett had to drive his wife over to Albert Park to see her daughter, on Thursdays that he was free for an hour or two from her observation or more than casual enquiry, on Thursdays that he could wander about the district while waiting for his wife and have no difficulty in explaining himself if seen on the nights of the first two murders. For the third, the 'real' murder it had to be a Thursday, of course. So the dates of these murders did indicate something, unlike those of Jack the Ripper which in spite of scrutiny, yield no information at all. (They were April 2nd 1888, August 7th, August 31st, September 8th, September 30th when two women were killed, November 9th, December 20th, July 17th 1889 and September 17th 1889).

"Then another thing which pointed to Crabbett was, curiously enough, his possession of a car. I expect you noticed how few of those in any way involved were car-owners—it surprised me. Only, as far as I knew, Miss Cratchley the headmistress of St. Olave's, Turrell, Beryl Knapstick and Dr. Ribbing, in addition to Crabbett himself. I was convinced the murderer either used a car or lived alone in Crabtree Avenue, otherwise how could he so quickly remove his raincoat and other distinguishing marks, deposit them and go to the public lavatory? It was possible that if like Heatherwell or Slatter he was alone in a house he could drop them there, but it was far more likely he put them in the boot of his car. If I was right about Crabbett they probably remained there from one murder to another, as it were. Why not? In his state of mind he was above and beyond any possible suspicion.

"So this is how I think Crabbett worked. He had been planning his course of action for two years. 'He's always late. Or has been for the last two years. Seems to have gone sort of dreamy though I can remember him when he was very wide awake'. That was what his daughter told me about him. His plan did not seem to me so much brilliant as long-pondered and inflexible. I think he congratulated himself on it. No wonder he was 'sort of dreamy' when under every humiliation from his wife he had this delicious and undetectable revenge to contemplate.

"The first murder was the easiest for 'The Stabber' did not exist then. He waited among the trees at the top of the avenue until almost everyone had left the school. He may even have known from observation that Hester Starkey went on foot down Crabtree Avenue every evening and have waited for her perhaps on several previous Thursdays without getting the combination of circumstances he wanted—an empty street and Hester

Starkey alone. At all events he got this on February 8th and followed his victim as he had planned till she was passing the empty house, near which, I should guess, his car was parked. He laid the body in the garden as he had planned, took off his raincoat etc. and having given himself a glance by a street light to make sure that he bore none of the marks of Cain too obviously, he made for the public lavatory.

"The knife? Oh yes. Perhaps long possessed, perhaps purchased specially. It is not a very uncommon weapon. I think it will lead now to a conviction. Meanwhile, on that night, it was in the boot of the car with the raincoat and cloth cap.

"Crabbett had nearly an hour to pass and went to the Mitre. The landlord told me that at this time he came in once a week or so, but after his wife's death more often. That seemed very natural and ordinary information unless one counted 'once a week or so' too literally. Then, having had a couple of drinks, he went to pick up Hermione and drive her home. Perhaps—the suggestion is the merest supposition—perhaps she complained that he smelt of drink. If so, I think he was silent thinking how soon, how few Thursdays away, her turn would come.

"The next Thursday, however, he drew blank. No woman alone in Crabtree Avenue. But the following Thursday, February 22nd just as he was about to give up for the evening and meet his wife at nine o'clock, Joyce Ribbing came out of the Whitehill's house and made for Perth Avenue in which was her home. He was only just in time and had to leave her body in the nearest garden which chanced to be Goggins's. No time for the Mitre that night. He had a wash and brush-up and called for Hermione. 'Dad was always late'.

"He had been clever in using Crabtree Avenue for the first two murders. He foresaw that watchfulness and precautions would be concentrated there, though no one would doubt that the third murder, committed in the same way and in the same district, would seem to be by the same hand. He foresaw, moreover, that when he did not come for his wife on time she would eventually decide to 'teach him a lesson' as she had often threatened to do, and walk down to the bus stop. Miss Pilkin saw him waiting about for Hermione to emerge. 'I saw that he wore spectacles. His features were in the shadow of a cloth cap' she said and when I asked her if she had ever seen this man before she said 'I was conscious of some sense of semi-recognition. Perhaps I had known him in a previous incarnation'. She had in fact seen him a few hours earlier when dressed in his usual greatcoat and hatless, he had brought his wife to Salisbury Gardens. But not all Miss Pilkin's instincts were mistaken. 'I saw an aura of evil round him.'

"This time Crabbett did not wait to go to the public lavatory. Why should he, now that he had the house to himself. He disposed of the body and having changed his coat in the car returned to his daughter's house to call for his wife. Then he hurried home to raise the alarm when she did not appear. Within a few hours he was receiving sympathy as the husband of the Stabber's third victim and within a fortnight he had begun to spend the money, advanced to him by his wife's executors one supposes.

"Now comes an interesting problem. Had he already planned the murder of someone who was to appear to have committed suicide as the Stabber? Or was this, as I have been inclined to suppose an afterthought? It may have been in conversation with me that he first realized that someone with a motive might be sought. 'You can't discount motive', I said. 'Oh, I thought you could with a madman,' Crabbett replied. 'Not even then', I told him. It may be that from this moment he decided that he would establish the Stabber's identity in the way he sought to do. Yet there is one consideration against that. If he had no plan for the fourth murder why did he not at once dispose of the raincoat, the cloth cap and the glasses and disembarrass himself of the butcher's knife? It is a point which has yet to be cleared up.

"At all events he still had these articles and set about finding his victim, as we have seen. On the night he murdered Slatter I heard on the telephone from Chumside the landlord of the Mitre that he had been in deep conversation with Slatter, but I was in pursuit of what by then seemed to me almost certain proof—information from Heatherwell that it had been Crabbett who called on the previous night when he thought Heatherwell was alone."

"And did you obtain that information?" Dyke allowed himself to ask.

"Not in so many words because Heatherwell is a man who tries to keep his promises. But to my own satisfaction, yes. When Heatherwell realizes the importance of the information he will certainly give it. And the lavatory attendant will be able to pick Crabbett out on any identification parade. But you won't have much difficulty in getting evidence, Superintendent, as you very well know. Think of the juicy lines of enquiry you have. (But you *are* thinking of them.) The sleeping tablets. The knife. The raincoat, with its possible bloodstains still to be found under the microscope and perhaps traces of something which connect it with the boot of Crabbett's car. The cap—that alone might hang him. His flat and Slatter's lodge where I have no doubt you have already made discoveries. The spectacles. The clothes Crabbett wore, if he has not destroyed them.

"Yet I doubt if you'll need to work on these. If I read the man rightly you will have a most detailed and proud confession as soon as he realizes that you seriously suspect him. His belief in his own cleverness and invulnerability once exploded he will seek another outlet for his paranoia, and will boast freely of what he has done."

"If you read the man right," said Withers suddenly, speaking almost for the first time that evening. "If—but it is certain you do. You have read him all along with most uncanny skill."

"Bravo, Deene," said Mr. Gorringer beaming. "I join our Chairman of Governors in his congratulation. But there is yet one question I would fain ask. You warned both Slatter and Heatherwell, I believe. How did you know that the murderer intended to add this fiendish afterthought to his misdeeds?"

"I didn't *know*. But we all have a little of the murderer in us and I perhaps more than most . . ."

"You alarm me, Deene!"

"I mean that to investigate crime at all one must be able to put oneself in the place of the criminal, turning about in the rat-trap he has created for himself. That is what I did in this case and saw that he might mistake this for a way of escape."

"A most felicitous conclusion by which you were able to save Heatherwell's life."

"But not Slatter's," said Carolus.

Dyke made no comment, then or thereafter, but rather abruptly took his leave.

Six weeks later, when Crabbett had, as Carolus predicted, made a full confession and was awaiting the trial that would send him for a lifetime to Broadmoor, Carolus decided to pay one last visit connected with the affair, the visit he had promised to Eamon Starkey at the Crucible Theatre.

He drove there alone and found the posters changed now bearing the stark words "Exp 7 Rev *Oedipus Limbo* by Tho Wilk" in letters of green on a yellow background. Hy Nox was again near the booking-office, stroking his thin red beard mournfully.

"Yes," he said, "I remember you. Your name's Car Dee and you're a friend of Index Eleven, aren't you? He'll be out in a minute. He has only a small Exegesis in Execution One. Do you want to wait for him inside?"

"I'd like to buy a ticket."

"Not one left, I'm afraid. We're packed every night for this. It's great, great. Tho Wilk at his most terrific. You'll just be in time for the shattering interloc between Indexes One and Seven."

Carolus saw as he entered the auditorium that only one bema was illuminated, the one on the left. It seemed crowded with skinny torsos and beards where a number of men wearing only loin clothes moved in rhythmic patterns as they talked.

"Ancient Britons?" asked Carolus.

"No. Ciphers. Nullities. Non-Existences."

Two of them punctuated the talk of the others with periodic clashing of dustbin lids which they held as cymbals. Each wore a lavatory chain with the handle falling on his breast and the bema was festooned with toilet paper. The talk seemed to be of plumbing.

"The poetry of it!" sighed Hy Nox.

"Is it poetry they are speaking?"

"Emancipated, yes."

A woman in over-alls interrupted the Non-Existences. She was lanky and her hair fell in sticky-looking strings, so that she looked like an Addams character.

"Venus Anadyomene," explained Hy Nox.

"Is that why she's nursing a lobster?"

"Of course. You're beginning to get the idiom."

Suddenly the other bema became illuminated showing three seated figures dressed and be-wigged as judges.

"Why *three* judges?" asked Carolus.

"They're plumbers," explained Hy Nox severely and the Mutual Consciousness went on.

Eamon Starkey when he emerged seemed contrastingly sane and commonplace.

"Let's go over to the Wheatsheaf," he said.

Not until they had their drinks was any mention made of the matter which had first brought them together.

"So there was method in his madness?" said Starkey.

"That exactly sums it up," Carolus replied. "It was madness. But there was method of a rather hideous kind."

"And my sister was the victim of both?"

"Yes. Of the Stabber and of the wife-murderer. The only thing that can possibly be any kind of a remote sort of consolation to you is that he knew his job and death was instantaneous. In those two years of planning he learnt the nearest and easiest way to the heart."